"Keeping your distance from me is not going to change the situation."

Isobel blew out a frustrated breath. She wasn't afraid of him—only that her unwilling attraction to him might make her vulnerable.

"All right," she said, trying to sound confident. "Why did you say you had proof that Emma is your daughter?"

Alejandro regarded her narrowly. "Because I do."

"I don't believe you."

"No? Believe it or not, I had gathered that," said Alejandro drily. Shifting in his seat, he pulled a wallet out of his back pocket and flicked it open. And as he did so a small photograph dropped onto the seat of the lounger beside him.

The photograph fell face up, and Isobel's eyes were drawn to it at once. *Dear God,* she thought, *he has a picture of Emma....*

Welcome to the April 2010 collection of fabulous Presents stories for your indulgence!

About to lose his kingdom, Xavian will bed his new queen, but could she be his undoing? Find out in the first installment of our sizzling DARK-HEARTED DESERT MEN miniseries, *Wedlocked: Banished Sheikh, Untouched Queen* by Carol Marinelli. They're devastating, dark-hearted and looking for brides!

Why not enjoy two fabulous stories in one with *Her Mediterranean Playboy* by exciting authors Melanie Milburne and Kate Hewitt. Be seduced under the Mediterranean sun, where wild playboys tame their mistresses!

Isobel has never forgotten the night Brazilian millionaire Alejandro Cabral took her innocence, but when he discovers she had his daughter, he'll stop at nothing to claim her again in *The Brazilian Millionaire's Love-Child* by author Anne Mather.

Why not unwind with a sexy story of seduction and glamour—Xavier DeVasquez will have innocent Romy slipping between his sheets one more time in Helen Bianchin's *Bride, Bought and Paid For.* Sally must become Zac's mistress on demand or risk ruin in Jacqueline Baird's *Untamed Italian, Blackmailed Innocent!* And billionaire Lorenzo Valente vows to have his wedding night in *The Blackmail Baby* by Natalie Rivers.

Look out for the next tantalizing installment of DARK-HEARTED DESERT MEN in May with Jennie Lucas's *Tamed: The Barbarian King!*

The glamour, the excitement, the intensity just keep getting better!

Anne Mather

THE BRAZILIAN MILLIONAIRE'S LOVE-CHILD

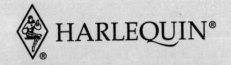

HARLEQUIN®

TORONTO • NEW YORK • LONDON
AMSTERDAM • PARIS • SYDNEY • HAMBURG
STOCKHOLM • ATHENS • TOKYO • MILAN • MADRID
PRAGUE • WARSAW • BUDAPEST • AUCKLAND

Recycling programs
for this product may
not exist in your area.

ISBN-13: 978-0-373-12909-6

THE BRAZILIAN MILLIONAIRE'S LOVE-CHILD

First North American Publication 2010.

All about the author...
Anne Mather

I've always wanted to write—which is not to say I've always wanted to be a professional writer. On the contrary, for years I wrote only for my own pleasure, and it wasn't until my husband suggested that I ought to send one of my stories to a publisher that we put several publishers' names into a hat and pulled one out. The rest, as they say, is history. And now, more than 150 books later, I'm staggered by what happened.

I had written all through my childhood and on into my teens, the stories changing from children's adventures to torrid gypsy passions. My mother used to gather these up from time to time, when my bedroom became too untidy, and dispose of them! The trouble was, I never used to finish any of the stories, and *Caroline,* my first published book, was the first book actually completed. I was newly married then, and my daughter was just a baby, and it was quite a job juggling my household chores and scribbling away in exercise books every chance I got. Not very professional, as you can imagine, but that's the way it was.

I now have two grown-up children—a son and daughter—and two adorable grandchildren, Abigail and Ben. My e-mail address is mystic-am@msn.com and I'd be happy to hear from any of my readers.

CHAPTER ONE

'Who is that guy?'

Sonia Leyton came to where Isobel was trying to stop one of the drunker guests from pouring another bottle of vodka into the punch and nudged her arm.

'Who is he?' she persisted, when Isobel seemed to be ignoring her. 'Come on, sweetie. You must know. You invited him.'

'Correction—Julia invited him,' said Isobel shortly, succeeding in blocking Lance Bliss from turning an already potent mix into pure dynamite.

'You're no fun,' he muttered, raising the open bottle to his lips and taking a generous slug. 'Lighten up, can't you? This is supposed to be a party.'

'But not a wake,' retorted Isobel, guessing what that amount of undiluted alcohol could do. 'Honestly, if I'd known.'

'You still haven't told me who that guy is,' protested Sonia, her mind fixed on a single track. 'You might not have invited him yourself, but it's your apartment. You must know who Julia asked to come.'

Isobel expelled a weary breath and glanced in the direction Sonia was indicating—though it wasn't entirely necessary. She'd noticed the man as soon as Julia had let him in. Their eyes had met very briefly, and she'd told herself the reaction she'd had was because he didn't look English. But the real truth was he was the most disturbingly attractive man she'd ever seen.

Tall and dark—younger than Julia, she suspected—with thick, straight hair that overlapped his collar and fell in a deep swathe across his forehead. She didn't know what colour his eyes were, but she was fairly sure they'd be dark too, complementing rather harsh features that were essentially masculine.

Right now, he was slouched on the window sill across the room, one lean, brown hand resting on his thigh, the other holding an open bottle of beer. But he didn't seem interested in the beer or the party, or in the woman whose arm was draped rather possessively over his shoulder.

'I don't know his name,' said Isobel now, wondering why Sonia didn't just go and ask Julia who he was. Though the answer to that was fairly obvious: Julia wouldn't like Sonia wading in on her territory.

'Damn!' Sonia looked disappointed now. 'I'm fairly sure I've seen him before.' She tucked her elbow into her palm and tapped her lips with a scarlet-tipped finger. 'Was it at the Hampdens' last week? Oh, but you wouldn't know,' she added, giving Isobel a rather scornful once-over. 'You don't like parties, do you?'

'Not parties like this,' agreed Isobel rather drily, half wishing she'd never agreed to Julia's request. But her apartment was so much bigger than Julia's flat, and it would have been churlish to turn her friend away.

'Oh, well, I'll have to go and find out for myself,' remarked Sonia, grabbing a glass and helping herself to a generous measure of the punch. 'Mmm; is there any alcohol in this stuff? It doesn't have much of a kick.'

Isobel shook her head, not bothering to answer. If Sonia

thought the punch was weak, she was obviously used to drinking a far stronger brew. Isobel knew for a fact that Julia had added a full bottle of rum to the mixture of wine and fruit juice she'd prepared. And that was only what she knew about. She wouldn't have put it past her friend to spike the punch with some other spirit.

Now, looking round the room, she could see quite a few of the guests were looking the worse for wear. She'd warned her friend that there were to be no drugs, but she had to wonder if some of the unsteady legs and glassy eyes might be due to more than just a surfeit of spirits.

The music, too, was definitely louder. Someone had substituted hard rap for the rock 'n' roll that Julia had chosen earlier. Watching the guests gyrating about the wooden floor, Isobel felt decidedly old, though she couldn't remember ever behaving so promiscuously, even when she'd been a teenager. And how sad was that?

Nevertheless, she had to live here long after the party was over, and she was well aware that her neighbours in this block of apartments in Mortimer Court wouldn't stand for it if the party turned into a rave. Her immediate neighbour, Mrs Lytton-Smythe, had already protested about the amount of cars blocking entry to the underground garage, and the two doctors who occupied the apartment below Isobel's had patients to attend to in the morning.

Julia had suggested Isobel invite all her neighbours to the party in an effort to defuse any objections, but that really wasn't a goer. None of Isobel's neighbours would have wanted to attend the noisy binge this was turning out to be.

Sighing, Isobel left the large room that served as both living and dining rooms in normal circumstances and headed into the small kitchen next door. The sound of music was less intrusive here, and she gazed at the debris of empty cans, wine bottles and the remains of the bought-in buffet Julia's guests had only picked at earlier. A glance at her watch told her it was already after midnight, and she wondered how long her friend expected the party to last.

Isobel was tired. She'd been up since half-past six that morning, trying to finish the piece about a well-known make-up artist that she'd promised her editor would be on her desk the next morning. Or rather *this* morning, she amended, wondering if she ought to have asked Julia to postpone her party until the end of the week. But today—or rather yesterday—had been Julia's thirtieth birthday and it would have been mean to deny her having it on the day.

Isobel sighed again as she turned, and then sucked in a startled breath at the sight of a man standing in the doorway, his shoulder propped against the jamb; it was the man Sonia had been asking about. He was lean and un-questionably sexy, in tight-fitting jeans and a black silk shirt, the sleeves rolled back over forearms liberally spread with fine, dark hair.

'Oh,' she said a little jerkily, unable to use his name because she didn't know it. 'Hi.' She paused. 'Do you need something?'

'*Nao quero nada, obrigado,*' he said, his voice low and disturbingly sensual. 'I want nothing,' he added, his accent spiking her nerves. 'I was looking for you.'

'Me!' Isobel couldn't have been more surprised. In the normal way, she had little in common with Julia's friends. She and Julia had attended university together, but for more than five years they'd seen little of one another, and it was only since Isobel had moved back to London that they'd renewed their friendship.

'*Sim*—you,' he agreed, with a smile that gave his words a disarming intimacy. 'I think, like me, you are—*como se diz?*—bored with these people, *nao?*'

Isobel frowned. So he was Portuguese, she thought, recognising the odd word in his language. But Julia wouldn't be pleased if she could hear what he was saying. She'd spent the whole evening hanging on his every word.

'I was just—tidying up,' she said at last, unable to believe he had come out here especially to see her. For heaven's sake, he didn't look the kind of man who'd be interested in someone so ordinary. She was attractive enough for a young woman who'd been married and separated all in the space of a couple of years, but she was certainly not a leggy blonde like Julia or Sonia.

'*Que?*' The man frowned. 'I do not believe you are just the—um—*domestico*.'

'Oh, no.' Isobel had to smile at that. 'This is my apartment, actually. Julia—your girlfriend...' It was hard to describe their relationship in those terms, she found, and why was that? 'She's a friend.'

'Ah.' He rested his head against the frame of the door for a moment, studying her with eyes that she now saw were an odd shade of amber. Framed by thick, black lashes, they caused a shivery feeling inside her, and she chided herself impatiently at the realisation that it was the first time she'd been attracted to a man since David had walked out on her.

He straightened and moved further into the room, and her eyes widened, half in apprehension, half with a sense of anticipation she'd never felt before. *Pull yourself together, Belle,* she instructed, deciding she must have sampled too much of the punch. But all he did was set the beer bottle he'd been carrying on the drainer, his lips quirking in amusement as if he noticed her not-so-subtle reaction.

Without going back to his original position, he paused and then said, 'So, you must be Isobel, *nao*?'

'Yes!' Isobel inclined her head a little breathlessly. 'Isobel Jameson.' She hesitated. 'And you are…?'

'My name is Alejandro. Alejandro Cabral,' he said, with a slight bow of his head. *'Muito prazer.'*

'Oh, um, how do you do?' Isobel was taken aback when he held out his hand towards her. She wasn't used to such a formal introduction, though she guessed where he came from the old courtesies still survived.

'I am very well, *obrigado*, Ms Jameson,' he responded softly, taking the hand she offered in return and raising it to his lips.

But, although Isobel half-expected him to touch his lips to her knuckles, Alejandro turned her hand over and bestowed a warm kiss to her palm. And briefly she was almost sure she felt his tongue brush against her skin, although she was so bemused by the whole incident she might well have imagined it.

She would have withdrawn her hand immediately, and scrubbed her palm over the seam of her cream cotton trousers and pretended the kiss had never happened, but he didn't let her go. Instead, he continued to hold her hand, gazing intently into her eyes. And she knew *he* knew he was disconcerting her, as much by his audacity as by her unwilling response.

'Mr Cabral…'

'You may call me Alejandro,' he interrupted huskily, and her mouth was suddenly dry. 'So long as you permit me to call you Isobel. That is such a beautiful name. My grandmother's name is Isobella. It is a very popular name in my country.'

Isobel ran her tongue over her dry lips, shaking her head half in bemusement, half in frustration. She didn't know where he'd learned his skills in seduction, but she doubted it was here. She guessed he was—what?—

twenty-five or twenty-six. And she was almost thirty. Yet he had a way of making her feel inexperienced and out of her depth.

'You can call me what you like, er, Alejandro,' she said. 'As long as you let go of my hand.' She managed to pull her fingers free and forced a smile. 'I gather you're not enjoying the party?'

He shrugged, broad shoulders moving sinuously beneath the expensive cloth of his shirt. 'Are you?' he countered, making no attempt to give her some space. He gestured about him. 'Is that why you are hiding in here?'

Isobel arched brows that were several shades darker than her honey-streaked hair. 'I'm not hiding,' she assured him firmly. 'If I were, I'm not making a very good job of it, am I?'

Alejandro regarded her between narrowed lids. 'We could hide together,' he suggested, putting out a hand and allowing a finger to trace the curve of her face from lip to jaw. 'Would you like that?'

Isobel took an involuntary step backwards. 'No. I wouldn't like that!' she exclaimed, impatient with herself now for allowing this to happen. Whatever impression she'd given, she wasn't interested in a one-night stand. Let Julia satisfy his libido. She had no wish to get involved with anyone else.

But unfortunately there was an empty crate positioned right behind her. Almost losing her balance, Isobel grabbed the counter for support, her fingertips accidentally brushing against the taut muscles of his midriff. Immediately, she felt the rush of heat she'd known when he'd touched her a few moments earlier but, when he would have reached to steady her, she hastily put some distance between them.

'I think you ought to go back to the party, Mr Cabral,'

she said, despite the fact that she'd called him Alejandro already. 'I'm sure Julia must be wondering where you are.'

'And that is of importance why?' he queried, his tone deepening intimately.

'Well, because it's probably very important to Julia,' said Isobel tersely. Then, in an effort to lighten the conversation, 'I expect you have lots of parties in Portugal.'

He shrugged, moving back to spread his arms along the counter behind him. 'I do not have parties in Portugal,' he remarked drily. 'I am not Portuguese. I am Brazilian.'

Isobel's lips parted, and for a moment she forgot her ankle, stinging courtesy of the beer crate, and the fact that she'd been trying to send him away. Her eyes widening, she said, 'How fascinating! I've always wanted to visit South America.'

'*De verdade?*'

She didn't know what that meant, but she hurried on regardless. 'So, are you working in London? Are you in advertising too?'

'Ah, *nao*.' His lips twisted mockingly. 'Advertising myself is not my thing.'

'I see,' said Isobel, though secretly she thought it was a pity. She could quite see him walking naked out of a foaming ocean, promoting some sexy fragrance for men. 'Um…so, what do you do?' she hurried on, afraid the direction her thoughts were taking might show in her eyes. 'Are you on holiday?'

'*De ferias?*' He sounded amused. And then, seeing her look of incomprehension, he explained, 'On holiday? In England—in November? *Acho que nao.* I do not think so.'

'Oh, well…' Isobel told herself she wasn't that interested, and reached for the bottle he'd discarded earlier. But it wasn't until after she'd snatched it up that she realised it was still half full. Beer splashed stickily onto her shirt and she was obliged to stifle an oath. 'Damn it,' she said, unable to resist the expletive. 'You should have warned me you hadn't finished.'

'*Muita pena!*' Alejandro pushed himself away from the unit and took the offending bottle from her unresisting grasp. 'I am so sorry,' he said, tossing it into the sink behind her. He gazed down at the damp fabric clinging to and outlining the lacy cup of her half-bra. 'What can I do to help?' His fingers moved to the buttons on her shirt. '*Por favor*, let me take this off.'

Isobel gasped in disbelief, smacking his hand away. 'What do you think you're doing?' she protested. His fingers looked so alien against the white linen. 'Don't do that! What if someone came in?'

Alejandro's mouth took on a decidedly sensual curve, but he obediently shifted his hands to the narrow bones of her shoulders. 'And that is the only reason you want me to stop?' he queried, those curious amber eyes burning with a golden fire. '*Muito bem.*'

Isobel found she was actually trembling, and it infuriated her. For heaven's sake, what was wrong with her? Even when she and David had first got together she'd never felt quite so vulnerable. Or so exhilarated, she admitted painfully.

'I think you should let go of me, Mr Cabral,' she said stiffly. 'I'm afraid you've got the wrong impression.'

'And if I don't want to?' he murmured, his thumbs probing inside the neckline of her shirt.

'I don't think that matters,' she retorted, refusing to let him see how he was disturbing her. 'I don't know what Julia's told you about me, but I'm not interested in casual sex.'

That shocked him. She saw the sudden darkening of his

eyes, the way the amber gave way to a much more sombre colour. But he still didn't release her. 'Nor am I,' he informed her flatly. 'And Julia has told me nothing about you. As surprising as that might seem.'

Isobel coloured. 'I just meant…'

'I know what you meant, *querida*.' His eyes impaled her. 'But somehow I do not think you are a virgin, *nao*?'

His fingers tightened a little and Isobel caught her breath. 'I'm divorced,' she told him shortly. 'Now, please—I'd like you to let me go.'

'Because I have offended you?' His scowl was absurdly attractive. 'That was not my intention.'

'No?' Isobel thought she knew exactly what he had intended. But right now she was more concerned with putting some breathing space between them. With his warm breath against her temple, and his fingers digging into her flesh, she was far too vulnerable. 'Well, whatever you meant, I'm not interested in massaging your ego.'

'My ego?' he sounded amused. 'So you think you know what kind of man I am?'

Isobel shifted in his grasp. 'I think you're too sure of yourself,' she declared stiffly. 'And, whatever you say, I doubt if you're a virgin either.'

He grinned then, white teeth showing between the sensual contours of his lips. '*Esta certo,*' he said. 'You are so right, *cara*. I have slept with women, *sim*. Would you like to know how many?'

'No.' She looked horrified now, and he gave a low laugh.

'I did not think so,' he said smugly, and, before she had an inkling of what he intended to do, he bent his head and caught the corner of her lower lip between his teeth.

He bit into the soft flesh, but the experience was more of a pleasure than a pain. His tongue stroked across her mouth, a sensuous exploration, and then his mouth covered hers and his tongue surged between her teeth.

One hand circled her neck, and she felt his fingers loosening the knot that bound her hair. She'd swept it up earlier, but she now realised how precarious it had become. Silky strands tumbled down about her ears and his knuckles, and his groan of satisfaction said it all.

Her muffled protest was only a half-hearted thing, the complete unexpectedness of what he was doing leaving her with an odd feeling of unreality. This couldn't be happening, she thought. Not to someone like her. David had always said she was frigid, but in Alejandro's arms the hot blood was fairly burning through her veins.

He moved so that she was pressed back against the counter, the hard strength of his body virtually moulded to hers. The kiss deepened and lengthened, and his hands sought her hips, bringing her fully against him, so that all thought of denying his love-making faded rapidly away...

'What the hell do you think you're doing?'

Isobel heard the angry exclamation as if from a distance. But its significance didn't register until sharp nails dug into her arm and she was wrenched away from Alejandro.

Then she saw Julia, and the look on her friend's face brought a damning feeling of shame. It took the place of what she described to herself later as utter euphoria; she was certain she must have been out of her mind.

'Julia,' she said, turning towards her. 'I—it's not what you think.'

'Isn't it?' Julia wasn't convinced. 'My God, is that blood on your shirt?'

Isobel half-wished it was, then she could claim that Alejandro had only been comforting her. But she doubted Julia would believe that either. 'It's beer,' she admitted ruefully. 'I spilled it all over me.'

'That's not all that's been all over you.' Julia was bitter. 'I thought we were friends, Issy.'

'We are—'

'So are you drunk or what? God, aren't there enough men here for you to choose from without hitting on my date?'

'Julia—'

'*Se fez favor.* Excuse me.' Alejandro had been silently listening to their exchange, but now he intervened. 'I came to the party alone, Julia,' he told her coldly. 'I may be many things, but I am not your date.'

'Oh, please—'

Isobel tried again, her gaze barely glancing off Alejandro's scowling face. She didn't dare look at him properly, didn't dare acknowledge something to him that she dared not acknowledge to herself.

Nevertheless, she registered his stillness, the fact that he'd pushed those long-fingered hands into the back pockets of his jeans. She could still feel those hands caressing her, she thought fancifully, but his expression didn't match her thoughts.

'We were together earlier!' Julia exclaimed, looking at Alejandro. 'You wouldn't be here at all if it wasn't for me.'

'I did not know your invitation came with—how do you say?—strings attached,' he retorted icily. 'You forget yourself, Julia. I do not need your permission to speak with Ms Jameson.'

'To speak with her?' Julia scoffed. 'Is that what you call it? When I came in, you had your tongue halfway down her throat.'

'And that concerns you how?' His accent was thickening, Isobel noticed. 'I suggest you leave us, Julia. We are not innocents who require you as a—a chaperon, *nao*?'

'Um—perhaps Mr Cabral should leave,' Isobel ventured, not looking at him as she spoke. 'It is getting very late.'

She heard his sudden intake of breath at her words. 'You do not mean this!' he exclaimed harshly, but before she could respond Julia intervened.

'She does,' she said, her expression triumphant. 'Bye bye, Alex. I'll see you next week.'

Isobel's gaze darted from Julia's face to Alejandro's. What was that supposed to mean? But he was already striding towards the door, and for a moment she thought he was going to leave without speaking again.

However he halted on the threshold, gripping the frame of the door with one hand, the other pushing back the tumbled darkness of his hair. 'This is not over, Isobel,' he informed her softly, and she didn't know whether that was a threat or a promise. '*Volto mais tarde.*' And what did that mean? '*Boa noite, senhoras.* Goodnight.'

CHAPTER TWO

AFTER Alejandro had gone, there was an uncomfortable silence. Then Julia said, 'That was fun, wasn't it?'

Isobel pressed her lips together. 'Yes, well, I'd rather not talk about it, if you don't mind.' She glanced down at her wristwatch, noticing the way her shirt was clinging to her, and cringing at the image she presented. 'It's late, as I said. Perhaps it would be a good idea if we wrapped things up now. It's after one, and—'

'You're not serious?' Julia's jaw dropped in disbelief. 'Issy, you can't. Things are just beginning to heat up.' She made an impatient gesture. 'Just because you got a little tight and made a pass at Alex, I'm not going to throw a wobbly. We've been friends too long to let a man—'

Isobel lifted a hand to silence her. 'How do you know him anyway? And what did you mean when you said you'd see him next week?'

'Oh.' Julia looked coy now. 'Didn't he tell you? Well, I don't suppose he had the chance, did he? We—that is, the agency—are doing some work for his company. Cabral Leisure is pretty big in South America. They're wanting to break into the European market, and our agency was the one they picked to promote them here.'

'Oh.' Isobel nodded. 'Oh, I see.'

'Yeah. Our Alex belongs in the big league, Issy. That was why I was so upset when I saw you two together.'

'Really?'

Isobel wasn't prepared to believe that, but Julia hurried on. 'I mean it, Issy. No one was more surprised than me when he accepted my invitation. I guess he must have been bored, yeah? Guys like him don't come slumming very often.'

Isobel turned away, gathering up the empty cans strewn about the worktops and dropping them into the waste bin. She was tempted to say that her apartment was certainly not a slum, but she didn't want to give Julia another excuse to patronise her. Besides, if he was as wealthy as Julia was implying, the other girl was probably right. At least, about him not mixing with the common herd every day.

'Anyway, just because he's walked out doesn't mean we have to ruin the party,' Julia continued when Isobel didn't bite. 'Another hour, Issy. Pretty please? Then I'll get the gang out of here, I promise.'

Alejandro walked back to his hotel.

It was a fairly warm night for London in November, which was just as well, because in his haste he'd left his leather jacket at Isobel's apartment.

It hadn't been a deliberate choice, he assured himself. He'd just been so angry when she'd asked him to leave that he hadn't thought about anything but getting out of there.

Now, the idea of seeing Isobel again intrigued him. As his temper cooled, he remembered her sweetness before Julia had interrupted them—the softness of her skin, the unexpected provocation of her mouth.

Isobel, he mused. *Isobella*. She'd certainly been different from the other girls at the party. Her almost shy manner reminded him of the girls back home, though he guessed Isobel had never had a chaperon breathing down her neck.

Except Julia...

His lips twisted. When she'd invited him to the party, he'd intended to decline. Although he'd been working with the agency, he wasn't in the habit of mixing business with pleasure. But she'd been so insistent, he'd eventually given in. After all, despite the wishes of his parents, he had no serious commitments elsewhere.

He scowled. He didn't want to think about Miranda at this moment. Not when thoughts of Isobel were foremost in his mind. She'd felt so good in his arms, warm, soft and sexy. He wondered how old she was. His own age, he guessed, but she looked younger. It was unbelievable that she'd been married and divorced. She seemed so innocent somehow. He knew he wanted to see her again. But would she want to see him?

Disappointingly, she wasn't at home when he called at her apartment the next morning. Instead, a garrulous old woman came out of the adjoining apartment and accosted him.

'Are you looking for Mrs Jameson?' she demanded, and Alejandro, who wasn't used to being spoken to in such a manner, felt his hackles rising. 'Anyway, she's not here,' the woman went on fussily, apparently unaware of giving any offence. 'She went out first thing this morning, though how she expects to do a day's work when none of us got a wink of sleep last night is beyond me.'

'Ah.' Alejandro was beginning to understand her reaction.

'Were you at the party?' she asked. Then, answering her own question, 'No, I don't suppose you were, or you'd not have expected her to be up yet.'

Alejandro didn't bother to correct her. 'You said *Mrs* Jameson, *senhora*. I understood the lady was divorced, *nao*?'

The woman's eyes widened suspiciously, as if she'd just realised he wasn't English, but she answered him anyway. 'She is,' she confirmed. 'Or that's what she told the landlord when she moved into the apartment.'

'I see.' Alejandro didn't allow his relief to show. '*Muito bem*; I will have to return later, perhaps, when Mrs Jameson is at home.'

The woman frowned at him through her thick-framed lenses. 'Are you a friend of hers?' she queried, and once again Alejandro had to tamp down his impatience. She pursed her lips. 'Who shall I say has called?'

Alejandro was fairly sure the question was purely curiosity now, and he was tempted not to reply. But the last thing he wanted was for Isobel to think he'd been snooping around. 'My name is Cabral,' he said shortly. Then, with a slight bow of his head, 'Thank you for your time, Mrs— Mrs—?'

'Lytton-Smythe,' she said at once. She paused for a moment and then ventured casually, 'Do you work for her uncle too?'

Alejandro hesitated. 'Her uncle?' he echoed, unable to prevent himself, and the woman nodded.

'Samuel Armstrong,' she said. 'He publishes magazines or something. Mrs Jameson is always on the go, interviewing famous people and writing articles about them for him.'

'Is she?' Alejandro was impressed.

'Yes.' There was reluctance in the woman's tone now, as if she regretted being so frank. 'I suppose she must be quite clever, really, even if it is only her uncle she works for.'

Damned with faint praise, thought Alejandro drily, but he was grateful for the information nonetheless. If only so he knew there was an alternative source to contact to get his jacket back, he assured himself. But that didn't alter the fact that he still wanted to see Isobel again.

Isobel was exhausted when she got back to her apartment. She'd managed to finish the piece on the celebrity make-up artist after the party was over, but it had been a good two hours after Alejandro Cabral had departed that she'd ushered the last of Julia's guests out of the door. Julia, herself, had left at least half an hour earlier, giggling with her bearded escort, fluttering fingers at Isobel and showing no remorse at leaving her friend to clear the place up.

In consequence, when Isobel did get home that afternoon, she still had to face the debris of the previous night's festivities. She had dumped the remains of the cold buffet into the sink-disposal before she'd gone to bed, but she'd been too tired then to start picking up the rest of the mess.

The first thing she did now was open all the windows. The smell of stale cigarette smoke and spilled beer was disgusting, and she leaned on the sill for a moment, taking in deep breaths of cool air.

There were scuff marks on the floor, she noticed, and cigarette burns on the arm of one of the chairs. But no ir-retrievable damage had been done. It could have been much worse, she assured herself.

Nevertheless, it took her a good half-hour to collect all the empty cans and bottles and drop them in refuse sacks for collection. Then, feeling she deserved it, she made herself a fresh pot of coffee.

Carrying her cup into the living room, she looked criti-cally about her. The floor needed waxing and the rugs needed vacuuming, but the worst was over. For now, she was grateful just to sit down on the sofa and close her eyes. She grimaced. The truth was, she wasn't used to such late nights.

When the doorbell rang, she was tempted to ignore it. She suspected it might be Mrs Lytton-Smythe, come to complain again about the disturbance she'd suffered the night before. Isobel had already had to apologise to the two doctors downstairs, whom she'd met on her way to the office. Thankfully, they'd been understanding, but her next-door neighbour was another matter.

Putting her coffee cup down on the low table beside the sofa, she got wearily to her feet. She'd kicked off her shoes when she came in, and she couldn't be bothered to look for them right now. Instead, she trod barefoot to the door.

It wasn't Mrs Lytton-Smythe.

But she had no difficulty at all in identifying the man whose shoulder was propped so casually against the wall outside. He was still as tall, dark and disturbingly good-looking as she remembered, even with a night's growth of beard. And a tremor of awareness feathered her spine.

'Oh,' she said, momentarily unnerved by his appearance. Her stomach hollowed and she pressed a hand to her midriff, trying to ground her scattered emotions. 'Hello.'

'*Ola*,' he greeted her softly, his voice as dark and sensual as molasses, with that distinctive accent that made everything he said sound like a caress. He straightened, dark brows lifting as he noticed her confusion. 'Am I disturbing you?'

Only totally, thought Isobel, swallowing to ease the dryness in her throat. 'Um—no. I just got in, actually.' She glanced behind her at the untidy living room. She couldn't invite him in. She just couldn't. 'Would you like to come in?'

Alejandro doubted she would appreciate his reaction at the moment. Going into her apartment had definite attractions—but taking her by the shoulders, crushing that tempting mouth beneath his own, pulling her close against his aroused body and letting her feel the response he seemed incapable of controlling was far more appealing.

He shook his head. This wasn't supposed to happen. Okay, he'd been attracted to her the night before, but he hadn't intended to pursue it. He'd wanted to see her again, yes, but not to feel this overwhelming need to touch her. For goodness' sake, what was wrong with him? His family would be appalled if they knew what he was doing.

However, Isobel had taken that rueful shake of his head at face value. 'Okay, then,' she said a little stiffly, misunderstanding him completely. 'How can I help you?'

'Nao!' Alejandro couldn't help himself. He spread his hands apologetically. 'I did not mean—*isto e*—I would very much like to come in.'

'Oh!' She was disconcerted now, but too polite to refuse. 'Okay.' She moved aside to allow him to enter, her hand fluttering towards the living room. 'I'm sure you remember the way.'

Alejandro stepped into the small entry, immediately dwarfing the hall. What had possessed her to do this? Isobel was asking herself. After what had happened the night before, she must be crazy. In the narrow confines of the hall, she was much too aware of him. As well as his size, which was intimidating, he was so disturbingly *male*.

When he looked down at her, Isobel felt as if she couldn't breathe suddenly. What now? But then he said, *'Voce primeiro,'* the words sounding absurdly sensual. 'After you, *cara*,' he added, and she realised she was letting her imagination run away with her good sense.

Somehow she managed to close the door and lead the way into the living room. But now the state of the apartment was the least of her worries. She was intensely aware of him watching her, and she wished she was wearing something a little more feminine than a cropped black tee-shirt and jeans.

And how pathetic was that?

'So,' she said when he halted in the doorway, looking about him with obvious interest. 'As you can see, I haven't had time to repair the damage yet.'

Alejandro shrugged. This afternoon he was wearing black jeans and a dark-green hooded fleece with the logo of some sporting club sprawled elegantly across the front. 'I did not come to check on the apartment,' he said, his golden eyes resting almost tangibly on her mouth. His brows drew together. 'You look tired, *pequena*. Did you not get any sleep?'

Isobel let out a breath. 'Gee, thanks,' she said, finding relief in sarcasm. 'That's so good for my ego.'

Alejandro's mouth compressed. 'It was not a criticism, *cara*,' he said, stepping towards her, and before she could restore the space between them he'd put out his hand and smoothed his thumb over the circles beneath her eyes. She blinked rapidly, her stomach plunging at the disturbing intimacy of his touch, and his lips curved in satisfaction. 'Relax, little one. Is it my fault that even your neighbour—Mrs Smith?—'

'Lytton-Smythe,' Isobel corrected him breathlessly, and his lips tilted.

'*Sim*; the good Mrs Smith,' he went on, ignoring her intervention. 'She complained that no one had had—what was it she said?—I wink of sleep, *nao*?'

Isobel couldn't help the smile that tugged at her lips at his deliberate corruption of the old lady's name. 'How do you know my neighbour's name?' she asked, backing out of harm's way. 'Did she speak to you just now?'

'This morning,' Alejandro amended, and to her relief he transferred his gaze to his surroundings again. 'This is a beautiful room.' He paused and once again his eyes drifted back to rest on her nervous face. 'Your husband— ex-husband, *nao*?—must have regretted having to leave.'

'He never lived here,' said Isobel swiftly. 'We lived, well, somewhere else.'

'But you do not wish me to know where?' suggested Alejandro shrewdly, and Isobel sighed. 'I think the memory is still painful, *nao*?'

'Not any more.' Isobel could be very definite about that. Sometimes she thought it had just been her pride that had been hurt rather than her emotions.

'There was another woman?'

He was persistent, and Isobel's lips flattened at the memories his words evoked. 'No,' she said flatly. 'Look, can we leave it? It all happened a very long time ago.'

Alejandro stepped towards her and now, when she backed away, she felt the unyielding coolness of the wall behind her. 'So,' he said a little roughly, 'are you still seeing this man?'

'What man?' Isobel gazed up at him blankly.

'If there was no woman, there must have been another man,' he explained harshly, raising one hand to rest it against the wall beside her head. 'I want to know if you are still—what is it you say in this country?—*with* him, *nao*?'

'No.' Isobel lifted a hand, as if she intended to ward him off. 'That is—all right, yes. There was another man. Now, can we please talk about something else?'

'You did not answer my question,' he said, his curious cat's-eyes searching her face with grim intensity. 'Where is this man who persuaded you to break your marriage vows?'

'Who persuaded me—?' She couldn't allow him to think that she'd caused the break-up. '*I* wasn't involved with another man. David—my husband—was. But it all happened a long time ago. Really, I wish you would forget about it. I have.'

Alejandro's nostrils flared. His reaction to the news that some other man had hurt her in this way was unbelievable. He wanted to find this man and give him the beating he so richly deserved.

Yet her relationship with her ex-husband should have meant nothing to him, he reminded himself. They were barely acquaintances. He had no right to care, one way or the other.

But he did.

Looking down into her slightly flushed face, he badly wanted to kiss her. Only the memory of the sensual heat her mouth had generated the night before, and the lack of control he'd experienced, held him back.

Even so, he couldn't prevent his need to touch her, and, lifting his free hand, he allowed one finger to trace a line from the curve of her cheek to her jaw. Nerves tensed beneath his touch. He could feel them, and there was an erratic pulse beating below her ear. He'd like to feel the source of that palpitation, to slip his hand beneath the tempting hem of her tee-shirt and stroke her breasts.

'Please…' It was as if she sensed his distraction and wanted to divert it. 'I don't know why you've come here, Mr Cabral, but I really think you should go.'

'You do not mean that.' Despite the obvious get-out, he didn't take it. His eyes dropped to her mouth. 'We are just getting to know one another, *nao*?'

'So why don't you go and sit down?' said Isobel a little wildly. She had to get him away from her. 'Perhaps you'd like coffee, or a cold drink?'

'I do not want anything to drink,' said Alejandro a shade impatiently, resisting the urge to show her what he did want with an effort. His hand moved to her shoulder, his thumb invading the neckline of her tee-shirt and smoothing the fine bones he found beneath the cloth. 'You are such a *contradicao*—a contradiction—*querida*. You say you have been married and divorced, *nao*? You admit your husband cheated on you, yet you seem—untouched.' His lips twisted. 'What kind of a woman are you?'

At this moment a desperate one, thought Isobel, her chest heaving. He thought she seemed untouched. She swallowed. Well, in a manner of speaking, she supposed she was. On the very rare occasions when David had had sex with her, she'd had to hide the fact that she'd felt nothing. Certainly nothing like the way she was feeling now. Was that why she'd never suspected that David had had another lover? Why it wasn't until the divorce that she'd learned the truth?

But Alejandro was waiting for an answer and she managed to say, 'A very confused one, I'm afraid.' She bit her lip. 'I'm sure you're far more experienced than me, Mr Cabral. Is that what you're trying to prove?'

'*Nao!*' Alejandro was annoyed, his eyes darkening with impatience. 'I wanted to see you again, Isobella. Is that so hard to believe?'

'Well, yes, it is, actually,' said Isobel, eager to keep him talking. 'I'm not the kind of woman you usually spend time with, I'm sure.'

Alejandro's jaw tightened. She was right, of course, though he was loath to admit it. Nevertheless, she did intrigue him, and that was a novelty for him.

His eyes dropped to the hectic rise and fall of her chest, and his jeans tightened instinctively. She had full breasts, high and rounded, and they were fairly erupting against the fabric of her shirt. Was she aroused, or was she apprehensive? Was that why she was pushing him away?

'Do I frighten you?' he asked abruptly, not sure where that had come from, and her eyes widened at the suggestion.

'No,' she denied hotly. 'But I'd still like to know why you've come here. I told you last night that I wasn't interested in—in—'

'Casual sex,' he interposed softly, bending his head to blow gently into her ear. 'Did I say that was what I wanted?' His mouth tilted at the corners. 'Oh, Mrs Jameson, I fear you have a one-track mind.'

Isobel decided she'd had enough. He might be right that she was a contradiction, but he couldn't know how inexperienced she was when it came to sex.

Raising both hands, she pushed hard against his chest, unbalancing him. Then, she jackknifed away behind the sofa.

But not quickly enough.

His hand caught her wrist, catapulting her back against him. The involuntary recoil brought her up against his chest, her breasts crushed almost painfully between them.

And not just her breasts, she realised, feeling the sudden pressure of his pelvis against her. A pressure reinforced by the swollen thrust of his erection, its heat throbbing hotly against her stomach.

But all this happened almost subliminally. Consciously she was drowning in the unexpected fire in his eyes. A fire that spread throughout her body, creating havoc in its wake. She felt as if she was being consumed, body and soul.

'*Querida...*' The word slipped helplessly from Alejandro's lips, his hand finding the nape of her neck and turning her face up to his. 'Do not—do not tell me you do not want me to kiss you. I think you want this just as much as I do.'

And then his mouth was fastened to hers, sucking all the breath from her body. Her lips parted beneath his, his fingers plunging into her hair. Desire, hot and electrifying, assaulted her senses. It was like a flame, licking along her veins, his tongue forcing its way between her teeth to possess the moist cavern of her mouth.

Alejandro's senses swam. This was not meant to happen, he told himself, yet the smell, the feel and the taste of her caused him to gather her even closer into his arms.

One hand traced the contours of her spine, cupping her bottom and lifting her against him. She couldn't fail to recognise what was happening. Almost without his own volition, he had surrendered to a need greater than his will.

And then the doorbell rang…

'*Cristo!*' Alejandro swore angrily, burying his face in the moist hollow of her throat, his overnight stubble abrading her skin. 'Do not move,' he groaned, uncaring of the reprieve this was offering him. '*Por favor*, Isobella, do not answer the door.'

'I must.'

Isobel had already slid away from him, tugging down the hem of her tee-shirt, lifting a trembling hand to push back the tumbled mass of her hair. Her voice was shaky, but it was determined. Like it or not, she was going to open the door.

CHAPTER THREE

'So, how did the party go?'

It was the following morning when the phone rang. Isobel had half-expected it to be Alejandro. Had half-hoped, if she was honest, even though he didn't have her number. But she'd found his leather jacket after he'd left the day before, and, although she suspected that was the real reason he'd come here, she desperately wanted to speak to him again.

But it was her Aunt Olivia.

Isobel's aunt and uncle had become her guardians when her mother and father had been killed in a skiing accident in Austria when she'd been only five, and she loved them as much as any parents.

'Um, it was okay,' she said lightly, but Olivia had detected the lack of enthusiasm in her voice.

'I did warn you, Belle,' she said ruefully. 'That crowd Julia runs with these days are not like you. What happened? Were there drugs?'

'No!' At least she hoped not, Isobel amended to herself. 'No, it just went on too long, that's all.'

'Hmm.' Her aunt didn't sound convinced. 'Oh, well, it's done with now. And I gather from what you say that there was no permanent damage?'

'No. No permanent damage,' Isobel agreed, wondering what her aunt would say if she told her what had so nearly happened the previous afternoon. If it hadn't been for Mrs Lytton-Smythe…

'So, when are we going to see you?' Olivia was speaking again and Isobel dragged her thoughts back to what her aunt was saying. 'You haven't spent a weekend at Villiers in ages.'

Her aunt and uncle owned a small estate in Wiltshire. Her uncle, who owned a string of magazines, commuted to London a couple of times a week to keep an eye on his editors, while her aunt bred horses and golden retrievers. Villiers was where Isobel had lived until she'd gone to university in Warwick and had met David Taylor, the man she'd married as soon as she'd got her degree.

'That's because Uncle Sam keeps me busy,' she said now, happier talking about her work. She enjoyed interviewing the various people who made the news and were interesting subjects. It might not have been her original career choice, but she appreciated the confidence her uncle had shown in her.

When she'd first gone to university, she'd intended to get a degree in journalism and then try to get a job with one of the national daily-newspapers. She'd had visions of becoming a war correspondent, sending back copy from embattled positions all over the world.

But meeting David, who'd been one of her tutors, had changed all that. Instead, she'd settled down with him in Leamington Spa, telling herself she was happy to work as a research assistant until they had a family of their own.

Of course, it hadn't happened. Instead, two years after their glossy wedding, she'd found herself lost and alone. Belatedly, she'd got a job as a journalist. But not in the way she'd ever imagined.

Now, though, her aunt sounded impatient. 'Then I shall tell Sam to stop sending you on all these assignments,' Olivia said firmly. 'It's time you found a decent man to look after you and settled down.'

'Been there, done that and no thanks!' Isobel exclaimed at once.

Even if it was six years since the divorce, she had no desire to get sexually involved again. She liked her life; she liked her independence. And just because she'd succumbed to a moment's madness the afternoon before…

'You're sure you've not met anybody?' Olivia persisted, and Isobel sighed. Her aunt could be far too perceptive at times. The last thing she wanted was to start a discussion about the opposite sex, particularly when her thoughts were so chaotic.

'No,' she said now, sinking down onto the arm of the sofa, hoping she didn't sound too adamant. 'So—how are things with you? Did Villette have her foal?'

'You know, I suspect you're trying to change the subject, Belle, but I forgive you.' Olivia's tone was dry. 'Anyway, moving on, why don't you come down this weekend? The Aitkens are hosting a dinner party to celebrate Lucinda's twenty-first birthday, and I know they'd love for you to join us.'

Isobel bit her lip. Apart from the fact that she and Lucinda Aitken had nothing in common, Lucinda's brother Tony would be there, and she knew her aunt and uncle had long nurtured hopes for her in that direction.

'Um—can I get back to you on that, Aunt Olivia?' she asked now, trying not to let her reluctance show. She hesitated. 'Maybe I could come down on Sunday, hmm? Just for the day.'

Olivia sighed disappointedly. 'I suppose beggars can't be choosers,' she said a little plaintively. 'Why don't you think about it, darling? Give me a ring tomorrow, yes? It's only Thursday. You may find you can come after all.'

Isobel felt mean, but she couldn't face Tony this weekend; she really couldn't.

But, 'Okay,' she said at last. 'I'll do that.'

'Good.' Olivia sounded infinitely more optimistic. 'I know you'll do your best, Belle. Oh, and for your information, Villette had the most gorgeous black colt. We've provisionally called him Rio, but you can choose his name when you see him.'

Rio!

Was there to be no escape from things Brazilian?

Isobel felt a reluctant smile touch her lips. 'I'll look forward to seeing him,' she said, and knew it was an unspoken admission as soon as she'd put down the phone.

Alejandro scowled when he found it was raining when he left the meeting. And, because it was the rush hour, there were no cabs to be had.

Sucking in a breath of cool, moist air, he turned up the collar of his mohair jacket and headed for the nearest tube station. He could have arranged for a company car to meet him, but he hadn't known exactly how long the meeting would last, and he'd thought a walk back to his hotel might be rather pleasant.

But not in the pouring rain.

Nevertheless, he wasn't used to so much inactivity. At home in Brazil, he walked, swam and sailed on a regular basis. And, when he wanted to get away from the city, he headed for the *estancia* his family owned in the beautiful country north of Rio.

Indeed, he sometimes thought he'd prefer to spend his days at the ranch rather than locked up in some stuffy boardroom. But, as the eldest son, he'd been expected to take control of Cabral Leisure when his father had retired. Roberto Cabral had been forced into early retirement after developing heart trouble, and he relied on both his sons to continue the development of the company.

His scowl deepened. He wasn't in the best of moods. Hadn't been in the best of moods, if he was honest, since he'd walked out of Isobel's apartment for the second time in two days in a state of raw frustration.

He could have gone back that evening, he supposed, but his pride hadn't let him. He'd consoled himself with the thought that the women he was used to associating with would never have invited a man into their apartment in the first place, not when they were alone. Particularly after the way he'd behaved at their first meeting. But she had, and he'd accepted, and now he was paying the price.

He shook his head, impatient with himself, impatient with the weather. Running down the steps into the tube station, he straightened his collar and ran a careless hand over his damp hair. The sooner he got back to Rio, the better he'd like it.

Got back to Miranda, he thought drily, although that wasn't a prospect he was looking forward to. He liked her; of course he did. They'd practically grown up together, damn it, but the crowd she ran with now was not his choice. Nevertheless, her mother and his father were making far too much of what was, in essence, a friendship. They expected an announcement, but they were going to be disappointed.

He forced himself to concentrate on the column of stations listed on the notice board. Yes, there was Green Park, on the Piccadilly Line, the nearest station to his hotel. But if he took the Central Line he was only a couple of stations from Isobel's apartment.

He blew out a breath. Okay, he told himself, why not take this opportunity to call for his jacket? He was leaving for home in a few days' time. This might be his last chance to collect it.

Yeah, right.

Did he really believe that was his only motive for going there? She'd shown him the way she felt on a couple of occasions already, hadn't she? Was he ready for another put-down?

In the event, he bought two tickets, deciding that whichever train arrived first would be the one he'd take.

Which meant that half an hour later he was climbing the stairs to Isobel's apartment, his jacket soaked and his expensive loafers oozing water.

She'd better be at home, he thought grimly, raising his hand to press the bell. It was a quarter to six. The working day was over. He could only hope she hadn't arranged to meet someone for a drink, or even dinner.

It seemed to take forever for Isobel to answer the door. A bit different from when Mrs Lytton-Smythe had called, he brooded irritably. But eventually he heard the bolt being drawn and the key turning in the lock, and presently he was given a glimpse of a bathrobe-clad figure sheltering behind the panels.

So she had an excuse for her tardiness, he thought, guessing she had just come out of the shower. Her face was flushed and her wet hair was in tangles about her shoulders. Well, what he could see of it anyway. She wasn't opening the door an inch further.

For a moment, Isobel just stared at him, too shocked by his appearance to think of anything to say. All she was conscious of was the fact that she was naked under the bathrobe, and tiny drips of water from her wet hair were finding their way inside her collar and down her neck.

'I was in the shower,' she managed at last, and Alejandro nodded.

'I can see that,' he said, those curious amber eyes intent upon her. 'Have I come at a bad time?'

You think?

Isobel's tongue sought her upper lip and she moved her shoulders uncertainly. Was this why she hadn't made any attempt to return his jacket? Had she suspected—no, *hoped*—that he might decide to come back?

'I suppose you've come for your jacket,' she said, deciding there was no point in pretending he might have another motive, and Alejandro arched his brows in a way that might have meant anything. He was more formally dressed this afternoon, in an elegant mohair-suit the jacket of which had been sadly impaired by the weather. His hair was almost as wet as hers, a thick, dark mass clinging closely to his scalp.

'You found it?' he queried softly, and Isobel's spine quivered at the dark tenor of his voice.

'Why wouldn't I?' she rushed on breathlessly. 'It wasn't hard to find.'

Alejandro inclined his head. *'E claro.'* Of course. He paused. 'So—you are well, *sim*?'

'A little cold is all,' admitted Isobel ruefully. And then, realising she couldn't go and get his jacket and leave him standing on the doorstep, particularly as he was obviously soaked to the skin, she murmured, 'I suppose you'd better come in.'

'If you are sure?'

Alejandro wasn't at all sure he knew what he was doing, but he'd virtually accepted her invitation now.

'Why not?' Isobel asked, a little offhandedly. And, unlike that other occasion when she'd stepped aside to let him in, she left the door to hurry into the living room. 'Close the door, will you?' she called, heading for her bedroom. 'I won't be a minute.'

Alejandro closed the door by leaning back against it. Then, turning, he flicked the key in the lock. For security, he told himself, refusing to admit he had any other reason. Then, as before, he walked into the living room.

The dark day meant there were lamps burning in three places around the room, two rather attractive table-lamps and a pewter standard-lamp with a huge, fringed shade. She had good taste, he conceded, noticing that the floor had been waxed and that the sofa and chairs had been thoroughly cleaned. Even the cushions bore no imprint of a human body, and the rug that occupied the centre of the floor looked like new.

A door was open across the room, and curiosity compelled him to find out where it led. But his jacket was wet and, slipping it off, he dropped it onto the floor. Then after a moment's hesitation he crossed the room and stepped into the short corridor beyond.

Evidently, the hall gave access to her bedroom and bathroom. There were two doors and, although he knew he was being unforgiveably inquisitive, he went forward towards the first door.

It was open, and was obviously her bedroom. He saw a rose-patterned bedspread and clothes laid out upon it. Was she preparing to go out? he wondered, unconsciously unfastening his collar as an unfamiliar twinge of something gripped his insides. He couldn't be jealous, he told himself, pulling his tie halfway down his shirt. It wasn't as if there was any way he could become involved with an English woman.

Yet...

Another door opened across the room and Isobel appeared, clad only in a skimpy half-bra and lacy briefs. She'd made an effort to dry her hair with the towel, but it was still curling wildly about her shoulders. She looked distracted, but amazingly sexy, and Alejandro felt his body respond.

She hadn't noticed him yet. She was too intent on picking up the filmy stockings from the bed and sitting down to roll them up her slender legs. But something, a sudden intake of breath on his part perhaps, caused her to glance in his direction.

With one leg raised so that he could plainly see the honey-gold curls escaping from the crotch of her panties, she was irresistibly appealing and, despite her gasp of outrage, Alejandro moved slowly into the room.

'What do you think you're doing?' Isobel could barely get the words past her lips, and, tugging off her stockings, she rolled them into a ball and flung them angrily in his direction. 'Get out of here!' she exclaimed, her voice rising half in panic, half in indignation. 'I—I asked you to wait in the other room.'

'As I recall, you did not make any—*como se diz?*—any stipulation, *nao*, as to where you wanted me to stay,' Alejandro contradicted her, huskily catching the ball of black silk in one hand and raising it to his face. 'Mmm, they smell of you,' he went on as she rose from the bed to face him. 'Do not be angry, *cara*. You are a beautiful woman. Do not be ashamed of your body.'

'I'm not ashamed!' Isobel caught her breath. 'But, if that's supposed to be some sort of apology, I don't accept it. You have no right to come here, uninvited, and behave as if I should be flattered.'

'It was not an apology,' inserted Alejandro mildly, dropping the stockings onto the floor and looking down at her with light, disturbing eyes. 'I was merely speaking the truth, *querida*. Do not blame me for that.'

'Oh, right.' Isobel glanced about her wildly, looking for something—her dressing gown, perhaps—to cover her semi-nakedness. But she'd taken her robe into the bathroom, and the trousers and sleeveless wrap-tank she'd been planning to wear offered little in the way of protection. 'And I suppose if I were a Brazilian girl you'd behave in exactly the same way?'

Alejandro's lips thinned. Despite recent events, he couldn't deny that there was no way Miranda's mother would have allowed him to enter her daughter's bedroom, even if he'd wanted to. Despite the new freedoms the twenty-first century had brought, women of good family clung to the old ways. Oh, that wasn't to say that young people didn't rebel. He was sure Miranda had done things her mother knew nothing about. But on the surface anyway the old customs applied, and he was honest enough to admit he'd want it no other way.

The silence between them stretched, and when he didn't answer her her lips twisted in contempt. 'I didn't think so,' she said, turning her back on him. 'Now, will you please get out of here?'

Alejandro's hands balled into fists, the urge to grip her shoulders and pull her back against him almost overwhelming. From this angle, he was offered only a glimpse of her breasts, but the narrow curve of her waist and the delectable swell of her hips were irresistible. And the rounded cheeks of her bottom protruding from the black lace of her panties sent a hot rush of blood into his groin.

He wanted her, he acknowledged grimly. Wanted to bury his burning sex inside her and expunge all the stress and frustration he'd felt since he first kissed her in the welcoming heat of her body.

But he couldn't do it.

He mustn't do it.

For God's sake, he wasn't an animal. And she wasn't some cheap whore he could seduce and leave without a backward glance. He respected her too much for that. And, for that reason, he had to get himself out of here before his own needs and the indisputable temptation she represented overcame his good sense

And then, as he was backing towards the door, she turned her head and looked at him. Blue eyes, as clear and lucid as a summer sky, met his tormented gaze. Eyes that softened and gentled as he looked at her, lips parting to allow the provocative tip of her tongue to appear between her teeth.

She held his gaze for long, disturbing moments, and then she said a little breathlessly, 'Your—your jacket's hanging on the stand in the hall. You—you might have seen it when you came in.'

In actual fact, Alejandro had been aware of nothing but Isobel when he'd entered the apartment, but he acknowledged now that there probably had been some coats hanging in the hall.

'*Certo,*' he said, a faintly mocking expression marring his dark features. Right. But what had he expected? he asked himself bitterly. That she might change her mind and beg him to stay? '*Obrigado.*' Thanks.

Isobel managed a slight smile over her shoulder, but her teeth came together and trapped her tongue before she could say anything else. He'd already shown her what he really thought about her. His silent admission that he wouldn't treat a Brazilian girl with the same lack of respect that he'd shown her proved it. Just because she was tempted to throw caution to the winds and let him make love to her—something she suspected they both wanted— she had to remember that was not a sensible option.

Alejandro had reached the bedroom door now, and before he stepped out of her sight he gave a slight bow of his head. 'It has been a pleasure knowing you, Isobella,' he remarked, not without some irony. '*Adeus, cara.* I hope you have a good life.'

As Isobel digested the finality of his words, he disappeared into the living room, and she waited breathlessly for the outer door to open and close. He was going, she thought, aware of her own mixed feelings about it. He had to go. But she didn't really want him to.

The silence was deafening, and her mood swung from ambivalence about his departure to an anxious curiosity as to why he hadn't left. She would have heard the door, she assured herself. Which meant he was still in the apartment. But why? What was he doing?

She had to find out and, snatching up the shirt she'd discarded when she'd gone for her shower, she pulled it on and wrapped the folds around her. It only skimmed her thighs, but at least it was a little less revealing than her underwear.

Alejandro was in the living room. Because her apartment was on the sixth floor, she hadn't drawn the curtains, and he was standing at the window staring out at the lights of the city.

He'd put on the jacket he'd been wearing when he'd arrived at the apartment, and she could see how wet and creased it was. Even so, that didn't explain why he was still here, and with a tentative clearing of her throat she said, 'Is something wrong?'

Alejandro swung round, his hands at his throat, and she realised he'd been fastening his collar and tie. She'd been too premature, she realised. She should have given him more time. As it was, she felt a fool for intruding.

'You have an interesting view,' he said, his hands dropping to his sides. 'My apologies. I realise I am overstaying my welcome.'

Isobel's tongue clove to the roof of her mouth. 'Your—

your coat's soaking,' she said at last, unable to think of anything else, and Alejandro's lips twisted.

'*Esta chovendo,*' he said, and then, collecting himself, 'It is raining, *cara.*' He spread his arms. 'When it rains, I get wet.'

Isobel pressed her lips together. 'You could—you could wear your other jacket,' she pointed out, and Alejandro's lips tilted.

'So I could,' he agreed ruefully, slipping the mohair jacket off his shoulders again. 'As always, you are—*como se diz?*—the soul of practicality, *nao*?'

Isobel didn't feel very practical, particularly when she was halfway across the living room before she remembered her state of undress. But by then it was too late to indulge in any false modesty, and, stepping into the hall, she lifted down the leather jacket she'd hung there and brought it back to him.

'Many thanks,' he said, coming to take the jacket from her, and as he did so she was made intensely aware of the damp, masculine scent of his skin.

'I—no problem,' she murmured. And then, before she could prevent the words, 'Your shirt's wet too.'

Alejandro lifted a hand and smoothed it down over his chest. The silk clung to his skin, and he made a slight gesture of acknowledgement. 'So it is,' he conceded with a rueful smile. 'Unfortunately, I do not have another shirt to wear.'

'I—I could dry it,' offered Isobel recklessly, and he gave her a conservative look.

'I think not, *cara.*'

'Why not?'

'You know the answer to that as well as I do,' murmured Alejandro, his voice thickening as his eyes lowered to the sensual beauty of her mouth. 'Or are you so immune to this attraction I feel between us that you do not care what I do?'

That was so patently untrue that Isobel could only stare at him in mute appeal. She'd never been more aware of any man, of his heat and his magnetism, and the indefinable aura of masculinity and strength that emanated from him.

'I—I care,' she got out at last, and she wasn't sure what she was admitting to when he cast his jacket aside and trailed an unsteady finger down her cheek.

'Merda,' he muttered, a low groan vibrating in his chest. Then his hand curled about her neck, and he was pulling her forward so that he could cover her mouth with his.

CHAPTER FOUR

ISOBEL gave an involuntary little gasp as he kissed her. The initially gentle pressure of his lips was so inviting, so insistent, and she couldn't help her hands from spreading weakly against his shirt.

Wet silk dampened her fingers as the satin-smooth heat of his tongue slid between her teeth and into the moist cavern of her mouth. The matching heat of his skin rose hotly through the fine fabric of his shirt, and her hands closed convulsively against the muscled pressure of his midriff.

He deepened his kiss, his hand sliding from her nape and into the tangled glory of her hair. His thumb explored her ear, finding the erratic pulse that beat so wildly beneath his touch, and he tilted back her head so that his mouth could seek the quivering column of her throat.

'I— We—we shouldn't,' she managed to stammer when she felt her shirt sliding off her shoulders, felt his fingers peeling down the straps of her bra.

'*Porque nao*? Why not?' he asked, using the words she'd used earlier. 'Do you not want me to show you what you do to me?'

'I just—' The erotic brush of his fingers across her breast caused her breath to hitch, and it was a struggle to remember what she had been going to say. 'Alejandro…'

'Do not tell me you do not want this just as much as I do,' he insisted, his accent more pronounced now, soft and sensual, soothing her shattered nerves with the downy brush of velvet. 'You do, do you not?' he persisted, circling her breast with his tongue, and she felt as if her whole body was on fire.

She moaned as his teeth took the place of his tongue and he took one swollen nipple into his mouth. Any lingering resistance was being eroded by his mouth and the intimate touch of his hands, and she wouldn't have been human if she hadn't responded to it.

Yet still she struggled to remember the reasons why she shouldn't let him do this. But, when his hand cupped the rounded swell of her buttocks and brought her close against him, the unmistakeable pressure of his arousal pulsing against her stomach caused her legs to turn to jelly.

'*Nao?*' he murmured. It was as much a question as a denial and Isobel felt her senses swimming.

'I—'

It was impossible to say the words she knew she ought to say, and, with a groan of triumph, Alejandro swung her up into his arms.

'*Quero*—I want you,' he said, burying his face in the hollow of her shoulder. 'Let me prove it, *nao?*'

His mouth found hers again as he carried her across the hall and into her bedroom. Her shirt and bra had disappeared and, apart from the scrap of black lace, she was naked in his arms.

Alejandro laid her on the bed, tearing off his own shirt as he came down beside her. He kissed her again as she fumbled with the buckle of his belt, and she turned towards him and cupped his face with her hot little hands.

The delicious provocation of her breasts against his

chest was almost his undoing. The urge to spread her legs and push his aching shaft inside her was almost irresistible, but he was determined she should enjoy this just as much as he intended to.

In Isobel's case, some coherent corner of her mind was still insisting that this couldn't be happening. She'd never been the kind of woman to sleep around and, apart from David, she was totally innocent of the ways of men.

Yet feeling him loosening his belt, unzipping his trousers, she couldn't resist trying to confirm what her subconscious mind was telling her could not be true. But the throbbing heat that thrust against her palms was all too real, all too powerful. He'd pushed his trousers down his legs, and his male strength was hard and unmistakeably aroused.

As she touched him Alejandro caught his breath, sucking air into lungs that suddenly seemed deprived of oxygen. '*Cara*,' he protested thickly. '*Cuidado!* Have a care! I have only so much control.'

Isobel's tongue circled her lips. 'But you like me to touch you?' she questioned, and he gave a strangled laugh.

'*Sim*, I like you to touch me,' he admitted huskily. But he captured both her hands in one of his and imprisoned them above her head even so. Then, his eyes darkening possessively, 'But I want to touch you too. Everywhere.'

Isobel trembled. Her whole body felt as if it was on fire with excitement and anticipation, and when he skimmed her lacy briefs down her legs she felt no sense of shame.

For the first time in her life she was glorying in her nakedness and Alejandro's reaction to it. With David, she had never felt like this, and it was only now that she really understood why.

Alejandro bent his head and buried his face in the soft curls of her mound, probing fingers seeking and parting the damp folds between her legs. She was wet, so wet and ready for him, he discovered half-guiltily. Why did he feel as if he was seducing an innocent? Why did he find that innocence so impossible to resist?

Isobel parted her legs almost involuntarily. The sensations Alejandro was arousing made her weak and eager for more. Even the scratch of his stubble against her bare thighs was unbearably stimulating to someone so inexperienced in the ways of sex.

It was difficult to breathe. The atmosphere in the room was hot and sultry. Just like Alejandro's love-making, the musky scent of his body was more erotic than she had ever dreamed. And when his tongue took the place of his fingers, penetrating those satin folds, she couldn't prevent the hoarse cry that issued from her lips.

She was on the brink of incoherence, mindless with need, aching to assuage the unfamiliar feelings inside her, when he lifted his head and covered her mouth with his. Then, straddling her thighs, he allowed the blunt head of his erection to nudge her tingling core.

'*Tu queria,*' he said thickly. 'I must have you, *cara.*' Then, with an ease she could only envy, he parted her legs and buried his throbbing shaft in her slick sheath.

He heard her catch her breath when his powerful thrust encountered tight muscles. *Deus*, he thought incredulously; it was almost like making love to a virgin. His contempt for her ex-husband was complete.

But when those same muscles expanded and then tightened around him his own urgent desire made any kind of intelligent thought impossible. Slipping his hands beneath her bottom, he lifted her so that he could encase himself completely. And, amazingly, she accepted him, her slim legs curving sensually about his hips.

When he started to withdraw almost to the point of separation she moved with him, and he heard her fractured breathing with a delight he'd never experienced before. She was the most responsive woman he'd ever made love with, and he wanted to prolong their shared quest for fulfilment as long as he possibly could.

But before long Isobel's eager response drove him to quicken the pace of his strokes. Her breasts were taut against his sweating body; even the little cries she was making were totally seductive.

He tried to hold onto his control, but he was fighting a losing battle. When the ripples of her climax caused her muscles to convulse around him and he was drenched with her essence, he had to pray she knew what she was doing. He couldn't hold out any longer, and with a final groan he surrendered to the blissful gush of his own release.

Alejandro's body had at last stopped shuddering and he rolled to one side so that Isobel could breathe more easily. Then a shrill sound assaulted his ears.

He heard the sound without association. Or maybe he just didn't want to recognise it, he realised. But as it continued he was forced to identify it as his mobile phone.

His face was buried in the pillows beside Isobel's head, and he wished with an urgency that bordered on paranoia that someone would just turn the damn thing off. But then he remembered that the phone was still secure in its own little pocket in his suit jacket. The jacket that was lying on the floor in the other room.

Stifling an oath, Alejandro pushed himself up onto his elbows and then jackknifed onto his knees.

Isobel stirred, casting languid eyes in his direction. 'What is that noise?' she asked, one hand reaching for his arm. 'What are you doing? I don't want you to go.'

'And believe me, *querida*, I do not want to go either,' he assured her huskily, capturing her hand and raising her palm to his mouth. His tongue briefly touched the soft skin, and then he added ruefully, 'My—how do you say?—my cellular telephone is ringing, *nao*?'

Isobel frowned. 'Your mobile?'

'*Sim*, my mobile,' he agreed, reaching for his suit trousers as he scrambled off the bed. Hopping on one foot, he managed to get his leg into one of the openings. 'You will excuse me, *querida*? It is no doubt my father, and when he calls and I do not answer he tells my mother and she worries, *nao*?' He raised apologetic brows. 'They both worry. They think London is a dangerous place.'

Isobel's lips pursed. 'Not that dangerous,' she protested, and Alejandro lifted his shoulders in a gesture of resignation.

'As you say,' he agreed drily, but, hauling up his trousers, he gave her a smile before striding out of the bedroom.

It was his father, as Alejandro had suspected it might be, but not calling to reassure either himself or Alejandro's mother that all was well with their son. He rarely rang, and only if the matter was urgent. This time the news he had to deliver caused Alejandro to close his eyes in frustration. It was a week since his father had made his first call on this subject. Now, although he had hoped to bring his son better news, it seemed the situation had got progressively worse.

'But can't Anita handle it?' Alejandro exhorted impatiently. 'For God's sake, Miranda is only nineteen!'

'Anita says she is at her wit's end. Your going away at this time has only exacerbated the problem. Miranda will not listen to either Anita or her counsellor.' His father paused. 'As I understand it, your final meeting was today, yes? I know you had planned to continue on to Paris, but I really think you should come home, Alejandro. If you care about the girl at all, you owe it to her to try and make her see reason.'

'I am not a professional, Papa.' Alejandro pushed agitated fingers through his hair.

'But you do seem to be the only person Miranda will listen to,' declared Roberto Cabral heavily. 'Please, Alejandro. Do not make me have to beg.'

Alejandro was closing the phone when he became aware of Isobel standing in the doorway. She had pulled on her shirt again, but it barely reached her thighs, and her feet were bare.

'What's going on?' she asked, her eyes puzzled, and he wished he had the right to tell her.

'It was my father,' he said, slipping the phone into the pocket of his trousers. He pulled a face. 'Regrettably, I have to return to Rio as soon as I can get a flight.'

Isobel's stomach hollowed. 'To Rio?' she said, feeling an awful sense of abandonment.

'I am afraid so.' Alejandro sounded as if he meant it, but what did she know?

'Is something wrong?' she ventured cautiously. 'Is your mother ill?' She couldn't think of anything else that might warrant such urgency.

'*Nao.*' Alejandro forced himself to brush past her without taking her in his arms again as he badly wanted to. 'It is a business matter,' he lied, going into the bedroom and rescuing the rest of his clothes. And, when she followed him to stand watching his hasty dressing, he added, 'Although my father retired some time ago, he still takes an active interest in the company's affairs.'

Isobel bit her lip. 'I see.'

Alejandro was sure she didn't see, but there was no way

without betraying a confidence that he could reassure her. Instead, he said, 'Do not look like that, *querida*. I want to see you again. It is just—'

'Business,' Isobel inserted flatly. 'I know.' Her lips twisted. 'You'd better hurry. I wouldn't want you to miss your plane.'

Alejandro finished buttoning his shirt and regarded her wearily. 'Do not speak so bitterly, Isobella. If there was any way I could get out of this *commitment* I would.'

'Yeah, right.' Patently she didn't believe him, and Alejandro desperately didn't want it to end this way.

'*Cara,*' he said persuasively, 'I will come back. To London, I mean. This is not the end for us, I promise.'

Isobel pressed her lips together and shook her head. She wanted to believe him. She really did. But for him to say he was leaving the country just as they'd become intimate seemed fated somehow.

'It doesn't matter,' she said, but Alejandro couldn't leave it like that.

'It does matter,' he said, pushing his feet into his shoes. 'I would not want you to think I do not care about you.'

'And do you?' asked Isobel between clenched teeth, knowing in her heart of hearts that he could say anything right now to appease her.

'Of course I do.' He regarded her intently for a few heated moments, because he knew if he touched her again he wouldn't be able to let her go. He added, 'Do not imagine I am unaware of my—responsibilities, *cara*.' A faint colour invaded his cheeks. 'You are right to doubt me. I have been—how do you say?—reckless, *nao*? I should have taken precautions, but—'

Isobel's cry of anguish arrested his words. 'Don't,' she commanded unsteadily. 'Don't say anything more. My God!' She gave a harsh gulp. 'I wondered where all this was leading. You nearly had me fooled, do you know that? Well, stuff your concern, *senhor*.' She used the title contemptuously. 'You don't have to worry about me. I can look after myself.'

'Isobella—'

'And don't call me that. My name is Isobel.' She gathered the folds of the shirt almost defensively about her. 'Just go, right? Before either of us says something we'll regret.'

'Isobel, *por favor*.'

'No.'

There was a break in her voice and she prayed he couldn't hear it. She would not break down in front of him, she told herself. She wouldn't! But she wanted to; she wanted to shout and scream and yell her feelings of betrayal to the skies.

Instead of which she marched stiffly to the door, refusing to look at him as he picked up both his jackets and followed her.

'*Querida*,' he said in an agonised tone, but she merely shook her head.

'Have a good journey,' she managed tightly, waiting for him to go past her. Then she closed the door and locked it again before allowing the hot tears to stream unchecked down her face.

CHAPTER FIVE

Three years later

FROM the air, the city of Rio de Janeiro was impressive: Sugar Loaf Mountain, the iconic statue of Christ on another mountain called Corcovado, and the glorious beaches surrounding Guanabara Bay.

Isobel had read that the earlier settlers had believed the bay was the mouth of a river. 'Rio' meant river, and, along with the month in which the country had been discovered, had given the city its name.

She'd read a lot on the journey, wanting to know as much about the country and its people as she could cram into the eleven-hour flight. She'd decided there'd be time enough to learn about her subject when she met her. She already knew Anita Silveira was a very successful writer. Having read many of her books, she felt she had learned a little of the woman's character already.

The irony of accepting the Brazilian assignment wasn't lost on her. Aunt Olivia hadn't wanted her to go, and even her uncle had had his reservations. But apparently Senhora Silveira had read some of Isobel's work and had asked that she conduct the interview. And, because it was such an important coup for *Lifestyles* magazine, Sam Armstrong had reluctantly agreed to let her go.

It wasn't as if she was likely to meet Alejandro Cabral, Isobel had protested when her aunt had brought the subject up. Rio was a huge city, with a population of well over six million. What were the chances of her meeting her daughter's father again? The odds were definitely stacked against it.

All the same, Isobel couldn't deny that she was looking forward to seeing the place where Alejandro had been born and where he'd been living when she'd known him. Their acquaintance had been so brief to have such long-lasting consequences, she thought a little bitterly. Yet she wouldn't be without Emma; her daughter had given real meaning to her life.

But now Rio was far behind her. When she'd arrived in the city two days before, Ben Goodman—a friend of her uncle, with whom he'd arranged for her to stay—had informed her that Senhora Silveira had retired to her coastal villa north of Rio. She apparently preferred the cooler ocean breezes of Porto Verde to the summer heat of the city.

Isobel didn't blame her. Having left London in the depths of a cold and wet January, she hadn't been prepared for the heat and humidity that had assaulted her as soon as she'd stepped out of the airport. In no time at all her cotton shirt had been clinging to her, and it had been such a relief to reach the Goodmans' house in the leafy suburb of Santa Teresa and discover it had air-conditioning.

Nevertheless, the beauty of the city hadn't totally escaped her. Despite the poverty of the *favellas*, there was so much she would have liked to explore: to ride the trolley cars and visit the many museums and art galleries, to walk along the beach at Ipanema and taste the vibrant nightlife for which the city was famous.

Still, she wasn't here as a tourist, she reminded herself

as the connecting flight from Rio to Porto Verde swept low over a high plateau, before descending with unnerving speed towards the coast. The small airstrip bordered the ocean; golden sand-dunes rippled beneath waving palms. In the distance, purple-fringed mountains looked remote and mysterious; nearer at hand the cliffs of the plateau gleamed white in the sinking rays of the sun.

Although Ben Goodman had never visited the Silveira villa, he'd told Isobel it was said to be very beautiful. She was a wealthy woman, he'd added without envy. A little arrogant perhaps, according to reports he'd heard, but also deserving of a little pity due to the fact that her only child, a daughter, had died when she'd been only twenty-two.

Not that her uncle expected Isobel to enquire into the woman's personal life. Anita Silveira seldom gave interviews at all, and she had only agreed this time because Sam Armstrong had been kind to her when her first book had been published many years ago. She didn't court publicity these days. She was a very private person. Isobel had been left in no doubt that she was extremely privileged to be given this opportunity.

The flight attendant passed along the aisle, informing passengers that they'd be landing shortly, and a few minutes later the small plane bumped down onto the runway. They taxied to where a cluster of iron-roofed buildings marked the terminal, the sea stretching away beside them, and no obvious security in sight.

There were only about a dozen passengers on the flight. This area of the country was popular with tourists, and judging by the shorts and backpacks, and the cameras slung about their necks, her fellow travellers were looking forward to their holiday. According to her guide book, the area offered trekking and climbing opportunities, while the huge Sao Francisco Lakes offered all kinds of water sports as well.

Once again, the heat struck her as she descended the steps from the aircraft. There was no jetway here, just a short walk from the plane to the reception hall. Then a rather longer wait for her luggage, and finally she grabbed the handle of her suitcase and emerged into the sunlight again.

There were taxis, and she had Anita Silveira's address, but this evening she was going to check in at a hotel and relax after her journey. She would make arrangements to see her subject tomorrow, after she'd had a decent night's sleep.

However, before she could approach one of the taxis, an elderly man dressed in a white shirt, a black waistcoat and baggy trousers came ambling towards her.

'Senhora Jameson?' he asked, showing a row of uneven teeth liberally stained with tobacco.

'Yes,' she said in surprise. 'I'm Ms Jameson.'

'Muito prezer, senhora.' Which must mean, 'pleased to meet you', Isobel thought as the old man commandeered her suitcase. He led the way to where an old-fashioned limousine was waiting. *'Entrar, por favor.'* 'Please get in'.

Isobel hesitated. Although she knew a few words of Portuguese, there was no way she could converse with him in his own language. And, although he knew her name, no one had warned her to expect an escort to her hotel.

'Um, who are you?' she asked politely, hoping he could understand her, and the tobacco-stained teeth appeared again.

'Manos, *senhora*,' he said at once, pointing a gnarled finger at his chest. 'I work for the *senhora, nao*? Senhora Silveira?'

'Ah.' Isobel was slightly relieved. 'And will you take me to the hotel?'

'Hotel?' Manos gave the word a Portuguese inflection. 'No hotel, *senhora*. You stay with Senhora Silveira, *sim*?'

Isobel's lips parted. 'But I thought…'

She frowned. What had she thought? Her uncle had said Senhora Silveira would arrange accommodation for her, and she'd naturally assumed she'd be staying in the small town. She bit her lip. Did she want to stay with a perfect stranger, however generous her offer might be? She always preferred to maintain her independence on these occasions. She found it made it easier all round.

But if there was no hotel…

'I—I don't know what to say,' she murmured half to herself, but evidently Manos heard and understood her.

'Por favor.' He gestured towards the car again, and this time he opened the boot and stowed her suitcase inside. 'Is not far, *senhora*. I drive ver' good.'

Isobel shook her head. She could hardly explain that it wasn't his driving that bothered her, not without getting embroiled in a conversation that probably neither of them would understand.

So, with a gesture of acceptance, she did as he'd asked and got into the limousine, wincing as her short skirt exposed her thighs to the hot leather of the seat.

Beyond the airport, the road wound along the coastline. The ponderous vehicle was surprisingly comfortable, which was just as well, because in places the surface of the road was rough and uneven. It was late afternoon, but the heat was still oppressive, and the old car had no modern amenities to counter the humidity.

'How far is it?' she asked at last as they drove through a small village, where colour-washed cottages with tiled roofs clustered round a small square. Barefoot children and lean dogs broke off what they were doing to watch the limousine's stately progress, and Isobel wondered if Anita Silveira enjoyed the superiority the big car gave her.

'Nao e muito longe,' Manos replied, his dark eyes

meeting hers in the rear-view mirror. 'Not far, *senhora*. You relax, *sim*?'

Isobel didn't feel very relaxed. She was still recovering from the long flight, and even Uncle Sam had been surprised when she'd phoned the night before to tell him she had to go to Porto Verde. Now the prospect of spending several days in the house of a perfect stranger was not appealing, and she half-wished she hadn't accepted the assignment and was safely at home with her little daughter.

She saw there was obvious development taking place along the coastline. She guessed that if she'd put off her visit for a few months there might have been a hotel where she could stay. Still, she was a stranger to Senhora Silveira too, and she'd been kind enough to offer her her hospitality. She should stop feeling sorry for herself and look forward to meeting the woman.

And then a wall of flowering trees on one side of the road gave way to an iron gateway. A small cupola topped the entry, and beyond a crushed-shell drive curved steeply out of sight. Manos swept the car between the gates with more enthusiasm than he'd shown thus far and accelerated up the driveway.

Isobel saw manicured lawns to left and right, before a screen of flame-trees exposed a pillared colonnade that evidently encircled the house. Arched windows on the upper floor gave the building a graceful appearance. Bushes heavy with blossom surrounded the forecourt, where a stone fountain spilled water into an orchid-filled basin.

The colonnade was shaded; it would be an ideal place to walk in the late-afternoon heat. Shallow steps led down to the forecourt where Manos first braked and then stopped the car.

Two men came down the steps on their arrival, dressed similarly to Manos, but much younger. One of them swung open the door for Isobel to alight, while the other went to rescue her suitcase from the boot.

Isobel was totally unused to this kind of treatment, but evidently Anita Silveira lived in some style, even at her seaside villa. Stepping out, she acknowledged the sense of tiredness that gripped her, half-wishing she was staying at a hotel and therefore was not obliged to greet her hostess tonight.

Then a woman appeared in the arched entrance to the villa, a tall woman of Junoesque proportions whose long, dark hair fell straight about her shoulders. She watched as Manos supervised the unloading of Isobel's luggage, but she made no move towards them, and Isobel wondered idly who she was.

Manos was at her side again and he gestured for her to go forward. '*O senhora* is waiting,' he said urgently, and Isobel realised this must be her hostess. With no choice but to climb the steps, Isobel was obliged to go forward. And as she drew nearer she recognised that the woman was quite beautiful: flaring cheekbones, a prominent nose, and a mouth that was both full and passionate.

There was a moment when Isobel thought she wasn't going to acknowledge her, that she intended to turn back into the villa and leave Isobel to fend for herself. But then, as if the moment had never been, she came to meet her, holding out her hand with all the regal assurance of a queen.

'Ms Jameson?' she enquired, as if there could be any doubt about Isobel's identity. 'Welcome to the Villa Mimosa, Ms Jameson. I am Anita Silveira, *e claro*. Come inside, please. You must be tired after your long journey.'

Isobel breathed a sigh of relief. She'd been half-afraid

that Anita might expect her to understand Portuguese. 'I am, rather,' she admitted, following the woman across the colonnade and into a square reception-hall. 'Thank you for allowing me to stay with you.'

Anita gave a careless gesture, clearly not considering that worthy of a response, and Isobel looked about her with interest: Dark-panelled walls, a tessellated floor, and sombre furnishings lit by a central chandelier. What natural light still remained was filtered through windows set high in the walls, illuminating sculpted alcoves and marble statuary.

The effect was rather daunting, but a bowl of white orchids occupying a leather-bound chest at the foot of the curving staircase provided a splash of colour. Arching doorways into adjoining apartments displayed rooms filled with heavy oak and mahogany furniture. There was a certain baroque quality about it all, totally different from Ben Goodman's home in Rio.

An elderly woman appeared from the back of the hall, clad all in black, her silvery hair confined in a severe knot. The housekeeper, Isobel guessed, noticing her snow-white apron. Another of the *senhora*'s servants. Isobel wondered how many there were.

After a low-voiced conversation with the old woman, Anita turned again to Isobel. 'This is Sancha.' She introduced them casually. 'Sancha looks after me and my home, wherever I am staying.' A smile touched her full lips. 'She is the *dona de casa*. If you have any questions while you are staying here, please address them to her.'

Isobel half-expected Sancha to shake hands too, but the old woman kept her eyes downcast. 'Sancha will show you to your apartment,' Anita added after another exchange with the housekeeper. 'She will also arrange for some refreshments, *nao*? The men will follow on with your luggage.'

'Thank you.'

Isobel was grateful for the respite. It would give her time to assimilate her surroundings and herself.

'Dinner is at nine o'clock,' Anita added, just in case Isobel thought she was free for the evening. 'Just ring for one of the servants when you are ready. They will show you to the terrace.'

'Thank you,' Isobel said again, and the other woman raised a hand in acknowledgement before disappearing through the archway to their right. The wooden heels of her sandals clattered across the block floor, before the sound of a door closing cut off any further sound.

At once, Sancha took charge. *'E por aqui,'* she said, her beckoning finger an indication of what she meant. With Isobel following, they passed beneath the arch of the stairs and out onto the veranda at the back of the villa.

After the coolness of the hall, the heat and humidity were intense, and Isobel wondered where the old woman was taking her. A cottage in the grounds, perhaps? Maybe employees of whatever persuasion didn't stay in the luxury of the villa. She wilted a little. She hoped, wherever it was, it had air-conditioning. Every garment she was wearing felt as if it was plastered to her skin.

In fact, her rooms opened off the veranda. Double-panelled doors gave onto a pleasant sitting room with a wood-block floor, leather sofas and several colourful landscapes on the walls. There was a marble fireplace—although when that might be needed, Isobel couldn't imagine—and a round, glass-topped table with four upright chairs. There was even a television, something Isobel hadn't expected.

The room was done with a much lighter touch than the main part of the villa, and Isobel turned to the housekeeper with a grateful smile. 'This is beautiful,' she said. 'Thank you, Sancha. I'm sure I will be very comfortable here.'

'*O quarto aqui,*' said Sancha obliquely, crossing the room and opening the door into an adjoining bedroom. Then, with an evident effort, 'Is good?'

'Very good. Um, *muito bem,*' said Isobel, hoping her schoolgirlish attempt at a response might win her a smile.

But Sancha only nodded as if it was nothing less than she'd expected. She let herself out of the room again as the men arrived with Isobel's luggage and her briefcase containing the laptop computer she'd brought with her.

She thanked the men, and was considering going for a shower when a maid arrived with a tray of refreshments: iced tea, hot coffee and a jug of fruit juice, as well as tiny sandwiches made from seafood and canapés oozing with caviar and cream-cheese.

Despite being certain that she wasn't hungry, Isobel found she couldn't resist tasting the delicious food. Like everything else at the villa, it was rich and sumptuous. She could get used to this, she thought drily. Or maybe not. She was simply too tired to think straight at the moment.

But not too tired to phone her aunt and uncle and let them know she'd arrived safely. She also wanted to hear about Emma. She missed the little girl so much when she had to go away.

'She's fine,' Aunt Olivia said reassuringly. 'She helped me feed the horses, and then we went for walk with the dogs. She's sound asleep now, probably dreaming about the puppies in the barn.' She gave a laugh. 'Not that she didn't ask at least a dozen times where you were and when you're coming back.'

Isobel's throat tightened. 'You will give her my love, won't you?' she said, a catch in her voice.

'Of course we will,' her Uncle Sam called over his wife's shoulder. 'Anyway, what's the hotel like?'

'Oh, I'm not staying at a hotel,' said Isobel quickly. 'The man who met me at the airport told me Senhora Silveira expected me to stay at her villa, so here I am.'

Her aunt was a little concerned that Isobel wasn't to be staying at a hotel where they could reach her easily, but her uncle wasn't alarmed. 'So what is it like at the Villa Mimosa?' he asked. 'Have you had a chance to talk to Anita yet?'

'Well, I've met her,' conceded Isobel, blinking back the tears that talking about her daughter had caused. 'She seems—very nice.'

'Do I detect a reservation there?' Her uncle's voice was more distinct now, and she guessed he'd taken the phone from his wife.

'Hardly,' protested Isobel. 'I'll let you know when I've had time to get to know her. I'd better go. This phone needs charging and I don't want to run it right down.'

She rang off and helped herself to one of the seafood sandwiches and a cup of coffee. The iced tea looked inviting, but she needed the kick the caffeine would give.

A maid arrived a few moments later and asked in broken English if Isobel would like her to unpack her cases. But, despite the temptation, Isobel assured her that she could do it herself.

She rested for a while after her shower, finding the queen-sized bed just as comfortable as she'd anticipated. But she was too hyped up now to go to sleep. Which was just as well, as she still had to unpack and decide what she was going to wear for dinner.

A little while later, she got up again and walked into the living room. The long curtains at the windows were not drawn, and she went to peer through the windows, turning on more lamps as she crossed the room. It was fully dark now, but lights had sprung up in the grounds of the villa. The glint of water seemed to indicate a pool, but it was too dark to be sure.

And then a shadow crossed the veranda outside. Immediately, Isobel drew back, half-alarmed. It was a man; she was sure of it. Had he been spying on her? She glanced towards the double doors in alarm. Goodness; she hadn't even locked them before going for her shower.

She considered opening the door and peering out, but that seemed foolish. Besides, when one of the palm trees outside swayed towards the windows, she couldn't be sure that wasn't what she'd seen before. She was on edge, she thought, anxious about her daughter and anxious about the upcoming interview. Once she'd had a good night's sleep, she'd view everything in a different light.

Returning to the bedroom, she quickly stowed her underwear on the shelves in the armoire. The few tops and dresses she'd brought barely filled the hanging space. Tank tops and shorts were folded into the drawers of the vanity, while the little make-up she'd brought with her looked lost on the cut-glass tray.

After several attempts, Isobel finally decided to wear a plain black slip-dress. It was formal without being too traditional, and was cooler than a sleeved top would have been. Strapless sandals, also in black, gave her height as well as confidence. But viewing the few pounds she'd gained since Emma was born was not the most reassuring thing.

The maid arrived so quickly after she rang that she was half-inclined to believe the girl had been waiting outside the whole time. Perhaps that was who she'd seen earlier, she thought. She hadn't been sure it was a man—or anybody, to be precise.

As soon as she stepped outside, Isobel was glad she'd worn the silk dress but the breeze off the ocean was appealing. It was the first time she'd noticed the scent of the sea.

Once again, they entered the main building, crossing the hall and through one of the immaculate rooms Isobel had glimpsed on her arrival. Beyond the room, a glass-walled terrace provided additional living space. And it was there that she found Anita Silveira, reclining languidly on a cushioned *chaise longue*.

She got to her feet at Isobel's entrance, however, her eyes flickering critically over the younger woman, making Isobel feel as if she was wanting somehow. Anita, for her part, was dressed in a flowing caftan of many colours, its dipping neckline and hip-high slit accentuating her voluptuous figure.

'Ah, Ms Jameson,' she said, putting down the cocktail glass she was holding and regarding her guest with guarded eyes. 'How delightful you look. So essentially English, *nao*?'

Isobel wouldn't have said so, but she supposed, compared to Anita's colourful outfit, she did look unexciting. 'I'll take that as a compliment,' she said, trying to make a joke of it. She glanced about her, noticing the waiter hovering over a chilled cabinet in the corner. 'This is nice. Less formal than—than—'

'You find my home formal, Ms Jameson?'

Anita leapt on her words, and Isobel decided she would have to think more carefully before she spoke. 'Um, traditional,' she said at last. 'It reminds me of houses I've seen in Portugal.' She moistened her lips and then continued, 'Actually, you have a very beautiful home.'

Anita looked a little mollified, and as if deciding there was no point in pursuing the topic she said, 'Let Ruis get you a drink, *senhora*. What will you have? Wine, perhaps? Or a cocktail?'

'White wine, please,' said Isobel gratefully. The last thing she needed was anything too alcoholic to confuse her already tired brain.

'Muito bem.' Anita snapped her fingers. 'Some wine for the *senhora*, Ruis, *por favor*.'

'Sim, senhora.'

Ruis sprang into action, and a moment later Isobel had a glass of white wine in her hand. 'Thank you,' she said as the young man resumed his position by the cabinet. 'This is very nice.'

Ruis bowed his head, and as he did so Isobel heard other footsteps crossing the room next door. They were slow footsteps, slightly halting, but Anita turned with evident pleasure towards the door.

'Ah, here is my son-in-law,' she said, startling Isobel, who hadn't known her daughter was married. 'Come and greet our guest, Alex. We have been waiting for you.'

Isobel expelled a sigh. She had wondered if Anita intended to start the interview tonight, and now she didn't know whether to be glad or sorry this wasn't so. Despite the hospitality she'd been offered, she couldn't deny she'd be glad when this particular assignment was over. And meeting members of Anita's family hadn't been part of the deal.

And then her legs weakened under her. The man who joined them was regarding her with a cool, sardonic gaze. Anita might know him as Alex, but Isobel was more familiar with Alejandro. It might have been three years and God knew how many miles since they'd last seen one another, but the man who stepped rather unevenly onto the terrace was undeniably her daughter's father.

CHAPTER SIX

ISOBEL badly wanted to sit down, but of course she couldn't. Not without drawing attention to her shocked expression anyway, and that was the last thing she wanted to do. Instead, she had to stand there with a stupid smile freezing on her lips while Alejandro crossed to where Anita was waiting.

She noticed, almost unconsciously, that he dragged one of his legs as he did so, and when he bent to bestow the expected kiss on each of Anita's cheeks, she caught her breath at the sight of the scar that scored a path from his right eyebrow to his mouth.

If Alejandro heard her gasp, he gave no indication of it as he greeted his mother-in-law. '*Ola, cara,*' he said, his voice just as low and disturbing as Isobel remembered. 'I see our guest has arrived.'

Our guest?

Isobel swallowed. What was she supposed to say now? Did she mention their previous acquaintance? In normal circumstances, she wouldn't have hesitated. But these were not normal circumstances, and she knew it. There was Emma to consider. Did he know about the baby? Or was this just an awful coincidence, as unexpected to him as it was to her?

Anita was speaking, and Isobel struggled to understand what she was saying. '*Sim*, this is Ms Jameson,' she heard the other woman say, stretching out a hand towards her. 'Come and meet my son-in-law, Ms Jameson—Alex Cabral. He is joining us for dinner.'

Before Isobel could say anything, Alejandro held out his hand in greeting. '*Bem vindo a* Brazil, Ms Jameson,' he said, which she knew from her phrasebook meant 'welcome'. 'It is a pleasure to meet you, *senhora*.'

So obviously he had no intention of acknowledging that he knew her. Isobel moistened her lips, wishing she could be as blasé about the situation as he was. Unless he didn't remember her, of course. She could be fooling herself that their relationship had been that memorable. He'd probably slept with any number of English girls on his visits to London. Remembering his reaction after they'd made love did not encourage her to believe it mattered either way.

And he'd evidently come back to Brazil and got married fairly quickly. Her fingers tightened on her glass. So, not memorable at all. But it was another fact to file away for the article she was going to write, she reminded herself tightly. Although she'd known Anita's daughter had died in her early twenties, she was fairly sure her uncle had never mentioned her having been married at the time.

Still, Alejandro had changed, she conceded. He looked much older than she remembered, but losing his wife was bound to have had some bearing on that.

Her stomach clenched, but she ignored it, concentrating instead on his injuries. Something had caused the flecks of grey in his night-dark hair and the deeply carved lines around his eyes and mouth.

Yet, for all that, he still possessed that soul-destroying

magnetism that had first drawn her to him. Even the ugly scar had added strength to a face that had always been wholly sensual, wholly male.

But it wasn't just his looks that caused her pulse to race so alarmingly. It was the knowledge that, if she wasn't careful, that subtle power he possessed might defeat her resistance once again.

Was he aware of it? Meeting those deep-set eyes, she had no way of knowing. His face was darkly intent, darkly perceptive, but also darkly enigmatic. She couldn't possibly guess what he was thinking at this moment. But the faint smile tugging at the corners of his mouth was unnerving. She suspected he was enjoying a joke—but was it at her expense or Anita's?

With an effort, she said, 'How do you do, *senhor*?' managing not to flinch when hard, slightly calloused fingers closed about her hand. But she couldn't prevent an instinctive recoil at the wave of heat that swept up her arm and into her face when his palm pressed briefly, intimately, against hers.

Oh no, she thought, meeting his gaze again and seeing the contempt that twisted his lips at her reaction. He thought she was repulsed by his appearance. Dear heaven, how wrong could he be?

And it seemed Anita was not indifferent to the silent battle of wills that was being waged between her son-in-law and her guest. Intervening, she said, 'Your uncle must have told you that my daughter, Miranda, died a little over a year ago.' Her eyes moved to her son-in-law, and she slipped an arm through his. 'Since then, Alex and I have become very close. Is that not so, *querido*? We survived her loss together.'

Isobel's eyes widened. She hadn't realised it was such a short time since Anita's daughter had died. But then, events moved fast in this part of the world, she conceded, trying not to feel bitter.

She wondered how long Miranda and Alejandro had been married, before—what? Had an accident torn them apart? Was it even possible that he'd been married when he was in London?

'*E claro.* Of course.' Alejandro was speaking now. If he objected to the older woman's possessiveness, he didn't show it. Then, addressing himself to Isobel again, his voice noticeably cooler, he added, 'I understand you have a daughter also, Ms Jameson. It is a pity you could not have brought her with you.'

Isobel suddenly felt as if the air-conditioned room had become airless. She couldn't breathe, and she was sure all the colour had drained out of her face. He knew, she thought unsteadily; he knew about Emma. But what did he know? Did he realise she was his daughter? How had he found out?

'I—I—'

The words stuck in her throat as she suddenly realised he hadn't been surprised to see her. She'd been so caught up with her own feelings, she hadn't identified the most important aspect of this meeting. He'd known she was coming. And for some reason he hadn't tried to stop her. Why? Why would he want to see her again? Unless Emma was the key.

Her mouth was dry, and she resorted to a gulp of wine to try and loosen her tongue. But all she succeeded in doing was choking herself, and she had to stand there coughing helplessly while Alejandro came forward and took the glass out of her shaking hand.

'I think our guest is too tired to answer your questions tonight, Alex.' Anita came to her rescue, and Isobel was grateful—although she couldn't help the ungracious thought that the woman had resented Alejandro's attention being focussed on someone else and not her. Turning, she snapped her fingers at the waiter, her instructions sharp and imperative, and he hurried out of the room. Then, with a tight smile at Isobel, she said, 'I have told Ruis to arrange with Sancha to have your meal served in your room, *senhora*. I am sure you would prefer it this evening, *nao*?'

Isobel's sigh was heartfelt. 'Oh yes; thank you, *senhora*,' she said, making sure to avoid Alejandro's eyes. 'I am rather weary. It's been a long journey. If you'll excuse me, I will have an early night.'

'I will escort Ms Jameson back to her suite,' said Alejandro at once, but to Isobel's relief Anita objected.

'I think Ms Jameson would prefer one of the servants to assist her,' she said, patting his sleeve reprovingly. 'She barely knows you, *querido*.' The smile she directed towards him was intimate. 'You can be a little intimidating at times.'

Alejandro's mouth thinned, and he said something to Anita in their own language that wiped the smile from her face. Then, turning to Isobel, he said coldly, 'I apologise if I have intimidated you, *senhora*. That was not my intention. We will continue our conversation at another time, *nao*?'

Isobel wanted to say that she had nothing to discuss with him, but this was not the time to start an argument, and she managed a polite smile in return.

'I'll look forward to it, *senhor*,' she said, refusing to let him see that he had rattled her. But she was overwhelmingly relieved when the maid who'd escorted her to the terrace appeared to escort her back again.

The food when it arrived didn't interest her. Isobel felt sick, disorientated, totally confused as to why she was here. Was she really expected to write an article about Anita? Or was that just a ruse to get her there? But, if that were so, what did Alejandro hope to gain by it? It all came back to Emma and she was scared.

It was still dark when Alejandro parked his SUV above the dunes that backed onto Anita's villa. He'd driven home after a rather strained dinner with his mother-in-law, rejecting her offer to stay over. But he hadn't gone home to bed. He didn't sleep well these days anyway, and after last night's little fiasco he hadn't attempted to undress. He was determined to see Isobel, to talk to her. And if that meant treading on Anita's toes, then so be it.

Running a careless hand over the growth of stubble on his jawline, he thrust open his door and got haltingly out of the vehicle. Despite the hour, the air was still warm, though there was a delicious breeze blowing up off the ocean. The scent of salt was stimulating, and he thought that in other circumstances he might have been considering taking his yacht out for a sail today.

The villa seemed all in darkness. Anita would still be sleeping; she rarely rose before eleven. Sometimes it was midday before she summoned Sancha to deliver the strong black coffee she drank so liberally. That, together with a narrow, black cheroot, was all she had for breakfast.

Which was why Alejandro occasionally chose this time to walk on the beach. His own property was a dozen miles from here, over a precipitous route that wound up into the hills above the villa. He didn't visit the villa every time he drove down here, but since he'd known Isobel was coming he'd begun to haunt the place.

It was hard, incredibly hard, to remain calm when he wanted to howl his outrage at the unfairness of fate. He hadn't realised it would be so difficult, seeing Isobel again.

And, while his situation had changed so dramatically, she seemed infuriatingly the same.

Except that she had had a baby…

The shadows lightened, highlighting a piece of driftwood in his path. Kicking it aside, he was grateful to avoid it. It would have been easy to mistake it for a clump of seaweed thrown up by the incoming tide.

Then, as he straightened, he saw her. It was still barely light, but there was no mistaking the slim figure etched against a sky lemon-tinged by the rising sun. His teeth clenched, and for a moment he wondered if she was just a figment of his imagination. But, no, she was there, her feet ankle-deep in the frothing water.

She wasn't aware that she was no longer alone. He'd allowed the SUV to coast the last few yards to where he parked, and the dunes muffled everything but the roar of the ocean. In shorts and a sleeveless vest, she was evidently not expecting to meet anyone. Perfect, he thought firmly. He'd wanted to catch her unprepared.

'Hi,' he said when he was near enough to speak without raising his voice, but she started anyway. 'Thinking of going for a swim?'

Isobel's hands came together at her waist. 'No,' she said quickly, glancing back towards the villa. Then, as if the thought had just occurred to her, 'Do you live here?'

Alejandro's lips twisted. 'No.'

'So did you stay the night?'

'Oh, please.' He swept back his hair with a careless hand, regarding her incredulously. 'Anita is my mother-in-law, not my lover.'

'Are you sure she feels the same way?'

The words were out before Isobel could prevent them, and she felt a moment's panic when his hands clenched into fists at his sides. What did she know about this man really? Despite that distant intimacy, he was as much a stranger to her now as Anita.

And yet…

'Does it matter?' His words arrested her troubled thoughts. Amber eyes darkened perceptibly. 'Are you jealous, *cara*?' His mouth took on a sensual curve. 'I must admit, it is an eventuality I had not considered.'

'In your dreams!'

Isobel's face flushed with colour and her eyes flashed in indignation. And Alejandro felt a frustrating twinge of guilt for making fun of her that way.

With the sun clearing the horizon, he thought how absurdly innocent she looked, her face free of any make-up, her lips parted and trembling. She was wearing pink this morning, and the clinging fabric of her vest exposed her nipples in minute detail. He doubted she was wearing a bra. In fact, he was sure she wasn't. And against his will—much against his will, he told himself grimly—he felt an unfamiliar hardening between his legs.

She turned now, evidently intent on putting some space between them, but he couldn't let her go like this. 'Wait,' he said, his fingers circling her upper arm as she would have hurried away. 'We need to talk, Isobella. Or are you going to continue with this pretence that you and I had never met before last evening?'

'I didn't start the pretence. You did,' Isobel countered, looking pointedly at his hand gripping her arm, and then up again into his dark face.

Alejandro frowned. He had to concede that she was right. He had made no attempt to tell Anita about that distant affair, and, although he'd been prepared for their meeting the night before, he hadn't taken into account how he would really feel when he saw her again.

'*Esta bem*,' he said shortly. 'All right. But would you

have rather brought up the subject of our daughter's paternity with Anita looking on? I think not. I think you were—how do they say?—shocked out of your mind when you saw me. And not just because of my changed appearance.'

'You're wrong!'

Isobel could feel the panic rising inside her. And she didn't honestly know why. Except that Alejandro's words threatened to expose her weakness. But Emma was her daughter, not his.

'Am I?' Patently he didn't believe her, and she hastened on.

'Naturally I was surprised to see you. I had no idea you and Senhora Silveira were related.'

Alejandro's mouth compressed. 'Now, that I can believe.'

'It's true.'

Isobel drew an unsteady breath. She wasn't handling this at all well, and it didn't help that the disturbing contrast between the dark fingers gripping her arm and her pale flesh was causing goose bumps down her spine.

If only she wasn't so aware of him. If only being this near to him didn't arouse memories she'd fought hard to forget. He hadn't cared what happened to her three years ago, she reminded herself. He'd left for Rio, and she'd neither seen nor heard from him since.

Taking another breath, she said stiffly, 'I came here to do a job, that's all. My uncle was delighted when Senhora Silveira's agent contacted him and offered the magazine this interview. He— Apparently he'd interviewed her many years ago, when her first book was published.'

'So why is he not here?'

'Because—' The dawning explanation stunned her. 'Because Senhora Silveira has supposedly read some of my work. Oh God!' Her eyes widened in disbelief. 'You arranged this, didn't you?'

Alejandro's mocking gaze neither confirmed nor denied it. Instead, he said, 'Did it never occur to either of you to question Anita's decision? She's a very private person, as your uncle certainly knows. And why, out of all the quality publications in the world, should she choose your uncle's magazine in which to break her silence?'

Isobel swallowed, trying to come to terms with what he was saying. 'Um, Sam thought she must have liked the piece he did about her before,' she said flatly.

'*Que nada!*' Alejandro's harsh exclamation revealed his contempt. 'I doubt if Anita even remembers what your uncle wrote about her.' He shook his head. 'No man in his position should be that naive!'

'He's not naive.' Isobel was indignant. 'Too honest, perhaps,' she added. 'Something I doubt you know anything about.'

'And why is that?'

Alejandro's fingers tightened round her arm, and she had to steel herself not to show any reaction. Did he know he was hurting her? Somehow she doubted it.

'You set up a totally bogus assignment and then ask me to explain?' Isobel chose her words carefully. 'I don't know what all this is about, but I shall make arrangements to return to London today.'

'*Nao.*'

Alejandro's response was very definite and her nerves tingled apprehensively. He was such a big man, strong and powerful. And, because of her unwilling awareness of him, he was a danger to her in so many ways.

Despite his scar, and the injury that caused him to drag his leg at times, he was still an overwhelmingly attractive man. It wasn't just his looks, though the muscles that swelled beneath his black tee-shirt and the corded length of his legs in black cargo pants were impressive. It was the hard-edged masculinity he exuded as he spoke to her. He knew what he was doing, and he was on his home ground.

Unknowingly, her eyes had strayed lower than she'd intended, and she unwittingly remembered the tight buttocks she'd once squeezed between her fingers.

Not that she should be thinking of such things now, she chided herself fiercely, refusing to acknowledge the unmistakeable bulge between his legs. But some things couldn't be forgotten, not when the reality was in front of her.

Oh, God!

He was waiting for her response, and she knew she had to keep her head here. He thought he held all the cards, but she had a few of her own.

'I wonder what your wife—or your fiancée—would have thought if she'd known what you were doing while you were in London,' she blurted defensively. 'I doubt if you told her, or your mother-in-law, that you were sleeping with someone else.'

'I did not have to.' Alejandro's face darkened. 'But we are not talking about Miranda, *querida*. This is all about our daughter. The daughter I did not even know I had.'

'How do you know she is your daughter?'

The words were out before Isobel could prevent them, and for a moment she saw she'd stunned him too. His fingers relaxed, and, taking advantage of the moment, she tugged away from him. And then, picking up her heels, she ran crazily towards the villa.

It was only as she was walking breathlessly across the formal gardens, where a lily-strewn reflecting pool lay between sprinkler-fresh lawns, that she glanced apprehensively behind her.

Her legs were wobbly, not just from the unaccustomed exertion, and she knew that if he'd followed her she wouldn't have the strength to repeat her escape.

But to her surprise, and relief, Alejandro was still standing where she'd left him. And she guessed that the reason he hadn't chased her was because he couldn't...

CHAPTER SEVEN

EVEN after taking a shower, Isobel didn't feel a whole lot better.

What was she going to do?

It was ironic, really. She'd spent half the night wondering what Alejandro was doing in this part of the country, and now that seemed the least of her worries.

Yet when she'd known him—if she had ever really known him!—he'd told her he lived in Rio, hadn't he? Perhaps it had been Julia who'd divulged that particular piece of information, when she'd been warning her that Alejandro had only been slumming at the party.

She should have listened to her friend, she mused unhappily. Julia had always been more streetwise than she was. Julia would never have let a man make love to her without using any protection. Even if Alejandro had probably assumed that, as she'd been married already, she knew how to take care of herself.

But that was just making excuses for him, something she'd done a lot of when she'd first discovered she was pregnant. Or had she just been finding reasons why she should have the baby? Even without her aunt and uncle's offer of support, she'd known she'd find some way to keep her child.

And now, it seemed, he was living in Porto Verde. Or if not here, exactly, then not too far away. Near enough for him to have contrived their meeting that morning. She should have asked him where his house was, she thought ruefully. But, right then, she'd had too many other things on her mind.

Not least what she was going to tell her uncle. He was going to be so disappointed when he learned that there was to be no interview after all. She dreaded having to tell him. He'd been so excited at the prospect of a possible scoop.

Wrapping herself in the pristine-white bathrobe hanging on the bathroom door, she returned to the living room. And found that in her absence someone had delivered a tray of fruit, rolls and coffee. The table had been set with porcelain flatware and silver cutlery, a napkin-wrapped basket keeping the bread warm.

Despite the appetising aroma of the coffee, Isobel looked about her rather apprehensively. She was sure she'd locked the door before going for her shower. But evidently certain members of Senhora Silveira's staff had keys. Did Alejandro have a key? She didn't even want to consider that.

When a knock came at her door, she started nervously. Now what? she wondered. Was this Anita's housekeeper, telling her she wasn't needed any more? But the fear that whoever it was might also have a key forced her to answer it. Putting down her coffee, she walked unwillingly to the door.

To her surprise, a young man was standing outside. Of medium height and build with handsome Latin features, he seemed very sure of himself. And, unlike the other servants, he was wearing a well-tailored grey suit, shirt and a matching tie.

'Ms Jameson?' he said expectantly, and Isobel wondered who else he thought she could be. But it did remind her that she was still wearing the bathrobe, and faint colour entered her cheeks at his frank appraisal. 'I am Ricardo Vincente, *senhora*—Senhora Silveira's personal assistant.'

'Oh.' Isobel was a little taken aback when he offered her his hand in greeting. 'Um, how do you do?' She hesitated, taking a surreptitious glance at the watch on his wrist. It was still barely eight o'clock. 'What do you— I mean, what can I do for you?'

She'd been about to say 'what do you want?', but she managed to bite the words back. However, after her encounter with Alejandro, she wasn't under any illusions as to why she was here.

'Ah. I am to escort you on a tour of the villa, *senhora*,' he said, his smile just the tiniest bit condescending. 'The public areas, *e claro*. Senhora Silveira's apartments are private, *naturelmente*.'

Naturally.

Isobel moistened her lips. 'And Senhora Silveira?' she ventured, hoping she wouldn't have to explain the question.

She didn't.

'Senhora Silveira does not allow visitors before midday,' Ricardo told her dismissively. Then, his eyes assessing her appearance. 'You would like me to come back, *sim*?'

What else? thought Isobel, a little irritably. As there was probably going to be no interview anyway, did it matter either way? Of course, Ricardo might not know what had happened. Had Alejandro explained the situation to his mother-in-law after Isobel had gone to bed? Or was that something else she had to look forward to—being humiliated in front of a woman who clearly had no liking for her.

But, 'Yes,' she said now, deciding that, short of making

a run for it, she was obliged to meet her hostess again. 'If you could give me half an hour. It is rather early.'

Ricardo arched dark brows. '*Mas*, the best time of day, *senhora*,' he assured her. 'Before it gets too hot.' Now he looked at his watch. 'I will come back in thirty minutes. *Ate entao, adeus.*'

'*Adeus,*' said Isobel, feeling a little foolish.

She was incredibly relieved when he turned away and she could close the door. She wondered when Alejandro was going to make his next move as the coffee she'd just consumed roiled unpleasantly in her stomach. If only she'd considered her aunt and uncle's reservations and let some other features writer take this assignment.

Yet, she suspected, that wouldn't have happened. If Alejandro had planned her involvement, he'd have found some other ploy to gain his own ends. She doubted Anita had been aware of the situation. Not before she got here, at least. Which might give Isobel a little leverage. Would Alejandro want to expose his duplicity to the mother of the woman he'd loved?

Who knew?

Alejandro was an enigma. She had no idea what he thinking, what he might do next. He'd changed. He wasn't the man she remembered. Was it something to do with the accident? Had he been responsible for Miranda's death?

She thought about ringing her uncle and telling him what had happened. She knew he'd be sympathetic. Once her aunt found out what was going on, she'd expect her to come home. But perhaps she should wait a little longer and see what happened. If Alejandro had his way, she suspected she wouldn't have a choice.

Alejandro flew back from Rio in the late afternoon.

There'd been a message waiting for him when he'd got

back from the beach to the effect that his father had called a board meeting that afternoon.

These days, Alejandro virtually ran Cabral Leisure himself. His father had had a stroke about eight months ago and he'd been ordered to take things easy from now on.

Not that Roberto Cabral had obeyed his physician. Despite Alejandro's success in creating new outlets for the company, Roberto insisted on attending all board meetings, making his opinion felt when he didn't agree with his elder son's ideas.

Just today, the extraordinary board meeting he'd called had been to question Alejandro's decision to install health spas in all their Latin American hotels. The hotels in the United States and Europe already had these facilities, and it was Alejandro's intention to give all their guests the chance to enjoy a healthier lifestyle.

Needless to say, his father's motion hadn't been carried. Even Alejandro's brother Jose, who didn't always see eye to eye with his older brother, had agreed that it was a necessary expense in these days of diet-conscious patrons. But it had taken Alejandro away from Porto Verde at a time when he'd had other problems on his mind.

Now, as his private jet began its descent towards the airstrip adjoining his ranch at Montevista, Alejandro acknowledged that, subconsciously, he'd spent the last eight hours fretting about what Isobel might do in his absence.

After that scene on the beach that morning, he'd been left with no illusions that dealing with her was going to be easy. But then, he hadn't expected to find her so attractive.

Despite his memories of his time in London, over the years he'd managed to convince himself that his attraction to the English girl had been as fleeting as their relationship. And, after his return to Rio and subsequent events, he'd never expected to see her again.

Had the accident never happened, would he have pursued the connection? There was no doubt in his mind that when he'd left London he'd intended to return within the next couple of months.

But, two months later, he'd been fighting for his life in the intensive-care unit of a private hospital in Rio. With a lacerated face, broken ribs, a punctured lung and the possibility that he might have to have one of his legs amputated, he'd been in no state to pursue any kind of relationship.

And by the time he'd got out of hospital and seen his injuries for himself...

The runway was partially illuminated by the lights from an off-road vehicle. Carlos Ferreira, his friend and stable-manager, was waiting for him when he stepped down from the plane. Between them they owned and bred polo ponies, thoroughbred animals that were sought after by many of the most famous riders in the sport today.

Alejandro's great-grandfather had built the ranch—or *estancia*—many years ago, and after the accident Alejandro had spent many weeks recuperating in the cooler mountain air. These days, it provided a welcome retreat from the demands of his work in the city. Since virtually inheriting the company he'd spent far too much time in Rio, in his opinion. And, as he'd always enjoyed riding, he found it was one sport he'd not had to give up.

Of course, since he and Carlos had started the breeding programme, the ranch had become very successful in its own right. Friends since university days, the two men trusted one another completely, and Alejandro was glad to leave all business decisions concerning the stud in Carlos's capable hands.

It was a relief to climb into the comfortable Lexus that

Carlos had brought to meet him—although his friend's news that one of their prize mares had aborted her twin foals was a blow. Alejandro knew that only about twenty percent of conceived twins made it to full term, but in this case they'd had high hopes of pulling it off.

'And Senhora Silveira has called at least half a dozen times,' Carlos continued, turning onto the rough track that skirted a stream. In the headlights of the car, Alejandro could see a handful of long-horned cattle wading in the reeds that grew in the marshes beside the water. 'I don't think she believed me when I told her you were in Rio. She wants you to join her for dinner this evening. She says she isn't happy about the interview.'

Alejandro swore, and Carlos offered him a rueful grin. 'The lady is persistent,' he agreed. 'Maybe this young woman you were telling me about isn't willing to put up with Anita's dramatics.' He chuckled. 'I told her you might not be back until tomorrow. Cheer up, my friend. Maria has made enchiladas for supper and you're invited.'

Alejandro scowled. 'Thanks.' He gritted his teeth. And then, almost to himself, 'I guess it is too late to drive down there tonight.'

'You'd better believe it,' said Carlos staunchly.

The road from Montevista to Porto Verde could be hazardous at times, especially after dark. A series of hairpin bends, the descent from the plateau where the ranch was situated was dangerous. And when it rained parts of the track had been known to wash away completely.

'In any case, it won't hurt her to wait until tomorrow,' asserted Carlos as a white-painted fence appeared ahead of them.

A gate in the fence guarded the lush paddocks where the horses grazed from the agricultural land outside. As well as horses, the ranch reared a herd of pedigree cattle, a few of whom they'd seen wading among the reeds earlier.

'I suppose not,' Alejandro agreed now, staying Carlos when he would have jumped out of the vehicle to open the gate. 'I can do it,' he added. 'I need the exercise.'

All the same, his leg twinged as he swung down from the Lexus. It brought another scowl to his face as he threw the gate wide so that Carlos could drive through.

Still, he thought after closing the gate and climbing back into his seat, if Anita was complaining it surely meant that Isobel was still there. He had been concerned that she might use his absence to leave the villa. Though, unless Anita had told her, she could have no real knowledge of where he might be.

He blew out a breath. He knew the child was his. He just knew it. It wasn't wishful thinking. Apart from anything else, the dates fitted, and there was no doubt in his mind now that Isobel's body had been nurturing his seed when he'd left England.

If only she'd told him. If only, as soon as she'd realised what had happened, she'd tried to get in touch with him. She could have reached him via the company's website. He was sure her friend—was her name Julia?—could have told her how to do that.

All right, perhaps he hadn't behaved very responsibly at the time. He wasn't particularly proud of his actions. And his father's phone call had created a difficult situation. After that, she hadn't listened to a thing he'd said.

They hadn't parted on the best of terms, and he'd left her apartment feeling gutted. All through the long flight back to Rio, he'd fretted over what he could have done differently. But he'd assured himself things would be different when he saw her again. He would make her listen to him. But a savage fate had intervened.

He still believed she should have attempted to contact him. He'd had a right to know, whether she'd wanted him to be involved or not. The baby was his child as much as it was hers—the only child he was likely to have, if the doctors who'd eventually discharged him from the hospital were to be believed.

A long drive edged by massive acacia trees led up to the main house. Two-storeyed, with white stucco walls and a railed balcony running across the front portico, even in the lights of the car it looked elegant and impressive. In all, the living area covered over half an acre, a wraparound veranda smothered with flowering vines giving the place a lived-in appearance.

Carlos brought the car to a halt on the block-paved forecourt, but Alejandro hesitated a moment before attempting to get out.

'Tell Maria thank you, but I'll take a rain check on the enchiladas,' he said, clapping his friend on the shoulder. 'But don't worry—I have no intention of driving down to Porto Verde tonight.'

Carlos regarded him doubtfully. 'You mean that?'

'Would I lie to you, old friend?' Alejandro countered, which wasn't quite an answer. He thrust open his door. 'Tell your beautiful wife I'll join you another evening if I may?'

Carlos gave a resigned grimace of acceptance, and with a farewell lift of his hand he set the car in motion again. Turning, he drove back to a fork in the drive and followed the gravelled track that led to his own house some half a mile further on.

Alejandro decided to take a shower before ringing Anita. It was a deliberate decision, a concerted attempt to prove to himself that he was still in control of the situation.

All the same, he didn't stop to dress before crossing the

vast expanse of his bedroom to where the phone extension was situated. His mobile phone was useless at the *estancia*. There was no signal, and they had to rely on the sometimes unpredictable land line to keep in touch with the coast.

Clad only in the towel he'd wrapped carelessly about his hips, he dialled the number, and to his surprise Anita answered the phone herself.

'Alex, darling!' she exclaimed, not without some annoyance. 'Where have you been all day? Carlos said you'd gone to Rio, but I couldn't believe it. You'd said nothing to me about going to the city when you were here last evening.'

Alejandro bit his tongue on a scathing retort and said instead, 'It was an emergency.' Then, disguising the irritation in his voice, 'Is something wrong?'

Anita chose not to answer his question, but said annoyingly, 'What kind of an emergency? Is your father ill again? Oh, I must speak to Elena. When I am away from the city myself, I am afraid I neglect—'

'My father isn't ill,' Alejandro broke in flatly, the chilled air from the cooling system bringing goose bumps out all over his skin. Or was that a sign of his apprehension? For God's sake, why didn't the woman get to the point? What was this all about?

'Then what—?'

'It was an emergency board meeting, right?' Alejandro knew he had to put a stop to her prevarication. 'Why have you been ringing me? I would have thought—um—Ms Jameson would have kept you busy.'

'Oh her.' Anita made a sound of irritation. 'I haven't seen Ms Jameson all day.'

'Why not?'

Alejandro only just managed not to bark the words, but he guessed Anita had caught the impatience in his voice.

'Well…' He could imagine she was pouting now. 'If it's

of any interest to you, I've had a migraine. But, after the way you left here last night, I doubt it matters.'

'Anita!'

'What?' she asked sulkily. 'When I couldn't reach you today, I was sure you were avoiding me. I know what Carlos said, but he's never liked me, and you know it.'

Alejandro sighed. 'Anita,' he said again, 'why would I want to avoid you?'

'Why indeed?'

Alejandro's free hand balled into a fist on his thigh. 'What's that supposed to mean?'

'Oh, please!' Anita snorted. 'I'm not a fool, Alex. I saw the way Ms Jameson reacted when she saw you. You were the last person she expected to meet. But you weren't surprised, were you, Alex? You knew she was coming.' She uttered an angry oath. 'I suppose that was why you persuaded me to give the interview?'

Alejandro stifled the retort that sprang to his lips and said levelly, 'I thought it was your agent who arranged the interview.'

Anita sniffed. 'Strictly speaking, I suppose it was, yes.'

'So why blame me?' Alejandro was dismissive. 'I thought you said that as well as talking about your writing you'd welcome the chance to lay some of the rumours about Miranda's, ah, problems to rest.'

'You say that so callously, Alex.' Anita clicked her tongue. 'She was your wife, you know.'

'Do you think I can forget it?' Alejandro's tone was bitter. 'But you know as well as I do that our *marriage* was a farce!'

'Don't say that!' Anita caught her breath. 'Miranda loved you.'

'Miranda loved herself,' retorted Alejandro flatly. 'Come on, Anita. Telling the truth won't hurt her any more.'

'Well, I don't think I want to talk about Miranda,' said Anita, sniffing again. 'Let the gossips say what they like. I don't care.'

She did, but Alejandro wasn't cruel enough to remind her of it. So far as his late wife was concerned, he'd had to cope with far too many demons of his own.

'Anyway,' she continued, 'why did Anton choose that particular publication?'

Alejandro avoided a direct answer. 'I believe you said you'd known Sam Armstrong when you first started writing.'

'I did, of course.' Anita was momentarily diverted. 'He was very nice to me.' But then she remembered her accusation. 'That doesn't alter the fact that the Jameson woman recognised you, Alex. Was it you who advised Anton to contact *Lifestyles* magazine? You might as well tell me. I'm going to find out anyway.'

'All right.' Alejandro blew out a breath. 'I did know who she was before she got here. We met some years ago, when I was in London. I—liked her. And, according to all reports, she's very good at her job. Why not have the best?'

Anita was silent for a moment and then she said silkily, 'And did you sleep with her?'

Alejandro's laugh was harsh. 'Goodnight, Anita,' he said grimly, and, holding the receiver with the tips of his fingers, he dropped it back into its cradle.

CHAPTER EIGHT

ISOBEL slept badly again and was up soon after six, gazing out at the shadowy silhouettes of the palms swaying beside the veranda.

She was waiting for the first trace of daylight to appear on the horizon, that tinge of pink that would rapidly turn to lemon-yellow as the sun began its morning ascent.

She wasn't dressed yet, but she would have loved to put on a vest and shorts, or even her swimsuit, and go down to the ocean. The water was so warm and appealing, and she longed to plunge her sticky body into the waves.

But the fear that she might run into Alejandro again was stronger. For the time being, at least, she would have to be content with taking a shower.

But she was so confused.

She'd spent the whole of the previous day waiting for Senhora Silveira to send for her, but it hadn't happened. Oh, Ricardo Vincente had taken her on a tour of the villa, as promised, and she'd duly admired the rich, if rather oppressive, opulence of its appointments.

But there'd been no sign of her hostess, or of Alejandro. Either the woman had changed her mind about the interview, or she was allowing her guest a little time to get over her jet lag.

As for Alejandro…

Isobel sighed.

As far as Anita was concerned, she couldn't quite believe she was that considerate. So what? Had Alejandro told his mother-in-law the truth? And, if so, had she pulled the plug on the interview? So why had Ricardo behaved as if she might be interested in Anita's background? When was anybody going to tell her what was going on?

The previous day had passed incredibly slowly. Although Isobel had her laptop with her, and she'd been able to edit an earlier article she'd written for the magazine, her heart hadn't been in it. Several times she'd gone into the bedroom and considered packing her suitcase, but pride wouldn't let her. She was here to do a job and, if she was permitted, that was what she had to do.

By the time she'd a shower and one of the maids had brought her breakfast, she was feeling a little better. Not optimistic, exactly, but prepared to face whatever was ahead. It was time that she showed some initiative. If Anita didn't know about Emma, there was no reason why she should change her mind about the interview.

Bearing in mind what Ricardo had said about Anita sleeping late, she delayed leaving her apartment until after eleven o'clock. But then, dressed in black-cropped capris that buttoned at the knee, a cream gauze-smock over a black vest, wedge-heeled sandals, and carrying a bag containing her recording equipment and laptop, she walked along the veranda and entered the hall of the villa.

It was already hot outside. Isobel could feel the beads of perspiration on the back of her neck. But the hall was cool and airy.

Two maids were using a power cleaner, polishing the mosaic-tiled floor. Her heels clattered on the tiles and attracted their attention. Isobel was about to try out her phrasebook Portuguese and ask where Senhora Silveira was, when a man appeared in the arched doorway across the wide expanse of the floor.

Tall and dark, with broad shoulders tapering to lean hips, the man's face was in shadow. But, even backlit by the sun pouring in through the windows of the room behind him, Isobel had no hesitation in identifying who it was.

Alejandro.

For a moment, her legs almost buckled. She hadn't forgotten the way they'd parted the previous day. But then, remembering her determination not to be intimidated, Isobel walked stiffly towards him.

'*Senhor,*' she said, using his title for the maids' benefit. 'I didn't expect to find you here.'

'Now, that I can believe,' remarked Alejandro drily, allowing her to make all the running. He leant his shoulder against the marble pillar that supported the lintel. 'How are you this morning, Ms Jameson?'

Isobel had to clear her throat before replying. 'I—I'm very well, thank you, *senhor*,' she said, halting a few feet from him. 'Eager to get started on the interview.' She hesitated and then continued, 'Do you know if Senhora Silveira is up?'

It was another of those ambiguous questions, and Alejandro's mouth took on a cynical curve. 'How would I know that?' he asked. 'I am not my mother-in-law's keeper. But, if you want to know why she did not send for you yesterday, I can tell you she was—what do you say?—indisposed?'

Isobel listened to what he was saying, but it wasn't easy. His nearness was too acute. Despite the fact that the scar on his cheek that had previously been obscured by shadow was now starkly visible, she was intimately aware of him. The power of his sexuality overwhelmed her, made a mockery of her intention to remain detached.

But, 'Indisposed?' she managed after a moment, and Alejandro inclined his head.

'She had a headache,' he said flatly. 'Anita's headaches are legendary. They appear at the most convenient times.'

Isobel concentrated on the neckline of his shirt, trying not appear interested in his explanation. 'Don't you mean *in*convenient times?' she questioned, and his lips curled with momentary amusement.

'I mean what I said,' he retorted drily. 'As you will find out in time, *querida*.'

Isobel shivered.

He was wearing a black shirt that clung to his torso this morning, smudged with sweat in places as if he'd been exerting himself in the heat outside. Black trousers clung to long, powerful legs, tight and revealing, the cuffs pushed into ankle-high suede boots.

'And do you think she'll be well enough to see me this morning?' she got out eventually, and sensed rather than saw the indifferent shrug that marked his response.

'She seemed all right yesterday evening,' Alejandro declared carelessly. 'But I doubt she will want to see you before noon.'

Isobel chanced a look at him. 'You were here yesterday evening?'

'No.' Alejandro spoke tolerantly. 'I spoke to her by *telefone* only.' There was a moment's silence, and then he added softly, 'I have been waiting for you, *cara*. I knew that sooner or later you would appear.'

Isobel expelled a breath. 'I thought we said all that needed to be said yesterday morning,' she declared, shifting her bag from one hand to the other. She glanced about her. 'Despite the *senhora*'s absence, perhaps you could tell me where the interview is likely to take place.'

Alejandro straightened from his lounging position. 'It

is not going to work, you know,' he said mildly, and Isobel felt the sense of panic she'd experienced when she'd first seen him engulfing her again. He hesitated, evidently choosing his words with care. 'But by all means take some time to consider the situation. I suggest we spend a little time together.' His brows lifted sardonically. 'You liked me once. I realise I have changed.' A rueful hand brushed his scarred cheek. 'Even so, perhaps I can persuade you I am not an unreasonable man.'

Isobel took an involuntary backward step. 'I—I didn't come here to spend time with you,' she protested, hoping the maids, who had abandoned their floor-buffing in favour of polishing the panelling, couldn't understand English.

'I know that.' Alejandro's lips twisted. 'But you don't have to be afraid of me. I may look like an ogre but, I assure you, I am still depressingly human.'

Isobel's eyes widened. She realised he had mistaken her panic for something else. 'You don't understand,' she said, her eyes darting towards his and then away again. 'I just meant I was asked to interview Senhora Silveira, and—'

'I understand what you meant very well, Isobella,' Alejandro retorted drily. 'And I also know why you were invited to come here. But surely it is not unreasonable in the circumstances to expect a little understanding on your part?'

Isobel's knees were trembling with the effort to maintain her composure. 'Are—are you saying there is to be no interview?' she asked. 'Because if that's the case—'

'Listen to me!' A muscle jerking in Alejandro's cheek betrayed his agitation. 'The interview is not at stake here. Do you understand me? Your association with Anita is your concern, not mine. What I would like to do is have a serious conversation with you about our daughter. I had planned to show you my *estancia* this morning, but—'

Isobel was distracted. 'Your *estancia*?' she echoed, and Alejandro sighed.

'*Sim*. My *estancia*,' he agreed, noticing she hadn't contradicted his other statement. 'My ranch, if you like. As well as my work for Cabral Leisure, I breed polo ponies.'

'Polo ponies?'

A faintly mocking smile tugged at the corners of his thin lips. '*Sim*, polo ponies. My manager does all the hard work, I am afraid. I just share in the rewards. It is my— *como se diz?*—my escape from the city, *nao*? You will like it, I am sure. But it is some miles from here, and since Anita was indisposed yesterday…'

His words reminded her of the situation, and she realised she'd allowed him to divert her with his talk of *estancias* and polo ponies. She also realised how little she knew about this man. Despite the comfort of her upbringing, she certainly wasn't used to the kind of wealth Alejandro seemed to take for granted. Perhaps he thought it would influence her.

But he was wrong.

'And did your wife like staying at the *estancia*, *senhor*?' she asked, deliberately bringing Miranda into the equation. 'I imagine she must have. Were you married as soon as you returned to Brazil?'

Alejandro's pale eyes hardened. 'Why would this interest you?' he demanded. 'Unless what you really want to know is why the accident occurred.' His mouth curled. 'Ah, you think Miranda would not have married me if it had happened before our wedding, hmm? You are suggesting that she must have regretted it? That that is why she overdosed on heroin within a year of taking her vows?'

'No!' Isobel was horrified at the emotions she'd inadvertently unearthed. She hadn't even known how his wife had died. 'That wasn't what I meant at all.'

'But I notice you do not deny that you find me repulsive,' retorted Alejandro bitterly. 'Still, I do not care what you think of me, *cara*—so long as you do not interfere with what I want.'

Isobel moistened her lips. 'Which is?'

'You know,' Alejandro told her heavily. 'I intend to get to know my daughter. To be a part of her life from now on.'

Isobel's stomach hollowed. It was what she'd been afraid of ever since meeting him again and realising the kind of man he was. A man used to having his own way, she hazarded. A man whose wealth and power would allow nothing to stand in his way.

Which was why she said desperately, 'I told you— Emma isn't your daughter.'

'But I know she is.' He was inflexible. 'I have proof.' Then, 'Be silent!' he commanded, when she would have protested again. Hard hands reached for her shoulders, forcing her to face him. And, although she glanced behind her, hoping the maids might come and help her, the two girls had slipped silently away.

'I had hoped we might deal with this as two adults,' he went on grimly, the hard pads of his fingers digging through to the bone. 'But clearly that is not to be the case. And that is all right with me also. I can be patient, Isobella.'

She winced then, and he wondered if he was hurting her. Alejandro acknowledged that he wanted to. Anger and frustration vied for dominance, and it was difficult to remain calm when so much was at stake.

For her part, Isobel was stunned by his assertion. What proof could he have? For God's sake, did anyone else

know about this? This was an Alejandro she hadn't anticipated, and something told her he wasn't about to be put
off with a futile denial.

She glanced up into his dark face, and then wished she
hadn't. Glittering amber eyes caught and held hers with a
riveting gaze. She couldn't look away, and unknowingly her
lips parted. Her tongue appeared again to moisten their
dryness, its pink tip giving her face a delicate vulnerability.

It wasn't meant to be provocative. Alejandro knew
that. But, as he continued to hold her, his earlier emotions
were giving way to something else—something insistent, and infinitely less controllable. An unwilling awareness reared its ugly head.

As on the previous morning at the beach, the memory
of how she'd felt in his arms overwhelmed his reason. He
still wanted her, he admitted incredulously. Wanted her
with an urgency that bordered on madness, his own needs
making a mockery of everything else.

When he jerked her towards him, she had no chance of
resisting him. She was caught off-guard, off-key and off-
balance. With a little gasp of alarm, she stumbled against
him, her case dropping helplessly from her fingers as she
tried to save herself.

But all she succeeded in doing was in fisting a handful
of his shirt to right herself. And, before she could draw
back, he'd bent his head towards her and captured her
mouth with his. The overnight stubble on his jaw only
added to his sexuality, and his hand at her nape sent crazy
shivers racing down her spine.

She sank against him, too bemused by the intimacy of
his actions to offer further resistance. The heat of his kiss,
the sensual possession of his hands, the clean, male scent
of his body were seducing her to a state where mindless
emotion was her only response.

He murmured to her in his own language, hoarse, unsteady words and phrases that she didn't understand. But their meaning was clear, and they only added to the sense of unreality that was gripping her, seducing her will and making her moan with pleasure.

His hands caressed her, sliding beneath her smock and her vest, spreading against the warm skin of her spine. She arched against him when his fingers traced the hollow above her bottom. And she felt the unmistakeable pressure of his manhood throbbing against her abdomen.

Alejandro felt his erection too. Felt his trousers tighten around him and the undeniable rush of blood to his groin. And knew a helpless sense of frustration at his body's weakness.

But the yielding softness of her hips against his was so good, so arousing. And the idea of burying his aching shaft inside her was a powerful thing. He remembered how tight she'd been, how satisfying it had felt to feel her muscles contracting around him. He'd never experienced such a sensation, like an explosion of his senses, of his will...

But no!

With a determination born of obduracy, Alejandro forced himself to lift his head and stare down at her. Her eyes were closed, and he briefly closed his own against the sensuous temptation she represented.

Her mouth was swollen, and there were marks on her cheek where the roughness of his chin had burned her. And, before he released her, he couldn't resist rubbing a possessive thumb across the abrasion on her skin. He wanted to do more—a lot more, he acknowledged with a certain amount of self-contempt. But time and their surroundings were against him. Besides, he had no intention of allowing her to think this gave her the upper hand.

That wasn't going to happen, he assured himself grimly. Forcing himself to put some space between them, he tried to quell the bulge between his legs with a slightly unsteady hand. *Calm down*, he told himself, grasping the pillar behind him. *However you feel, you've got to stay in control.*

His injured leg provided a distraction—albeit an unwelcome one. Standing for any length of time was unwise, and the muscles in his jaw tightened as a shaft of pain arrowed down his thigh.

Still, it reminded him of how unpredictable life could be. How unpredictable his own life had been to this point. *Meu Deus*, did he want her to think he was still attracted to her? She provoked him, that was all. To the point of madness at times.

Meanwhile Isobel had no idea what he was thinking. She'd opened her eyes to find him regarding her with an unmistakeable look of contempt on his face. Her face flamed instinctively, at the thought of her own stupidity, if nothing else.

She could console herself with the thought that the confusion he'd created in her mind over Emma had clouded her reason. But for a moment, while he'd been kissing her, she'd had to admit all her inhibitions about him and his intentions had scattered to the winds.

'Are you all right?'

The coldness of his voice was an added push towards sobriety and Isobel took a steadying breath. Then, bending to rescue the case containing her laptop, she said tersely, 'I will be. When I get out of here.' And, because it was the uppermost thought in her mind, she added, 'And please don't think I believe your lies. Or that by throwing your wealth in my face I'll be so overwhelmed with admiration that I'll submit to any suggestion you make.' She squared her shoulders. 'Now, if you'll excuse me?'

'Tomorrow,' said Alejandro, as if she hadn't spoken. 'We will go to Montevista tomorrow. I will pick you up at eight o'clock.'

Isobel blinked. 'Montevista?' she said, realising she was back to repeating everything he said. 'What the hell is—?' She broke off, annoyed that she had shown any interest. 'Well, whatever it is, or *wherever* it is, I'm not going anywhere.'

'Montevista is my *estancia*,' said Alejandro with infuriating calmness. 'As I said earlier, before you fell so conveniently into my arms...'

'I didn't fall into your arms.'

'You will like it. It is very beautiful. Very remote.' He paused. 'Please do not let me down, Isobella. I am not a wise man to cross.'

'Is that a threat, *senhor*?'

Isobel tried to sound defiant, but she could hear the tremor in her voice.

'It is my advice, *cara*. Eight o'clock, *sim*?'

'And if I refuse?' Isobel forced herself to meet his gaze. 'Will you force me, *senhor*?'

Alejandro's pale eyes hardened. 'I suggest you grow up, Isobella,' he said, his voice harsh with feeling. 'I realise my appearance is a deterrent, but you will get used to it. I can promise you that.'

'You really don't understand.' Isobel stared at him helplessly. 'Your appearance has nothing to do with it.' Then, because she was sure he didn't believe her, 'And pretending you can prove that Emma is your daughter—'

'I can.'

'No.'

'Yes.'

'What is going on here?'

The imperious voice was both a relief and a frustration.

Isobel sighed and turned to find Anita Silveira crossing the hall towards them. She was trailing the ties of a chiffon wrap that was open over a matching negligee, and Isobel had to acknowledge that only a woman of her arrogance and stature could manage to look elegant in such an unsuitable outfit.

'Alex!' she exclaimed, her eyes flickering over Isobel and then returning to him. 'Why are you here? I did not know you were coming. Come, we can have brunch together.'

'I am not hungry, Anita,' said Alejandro coolly, apparently not at all perturbed by his mother-in-law's appearance. 'As a matter of fact, I was just leaving.'

Anita's brows drew together. 'But you have been talking to Ms Jameson!' she protested.

'In your absence, that is all, *querida*,' Alejandro lied without apparent conscience. 'I was merely telling her about the *estancia*, *nao*?' He turned back to Isobel. '*Adeus*, Ms Jameson. It has been a pleasure. *Adeus*, Anita. We will talk tomorrow, *talvez*?'

'Wait!' Anita turned irritably to Isobel herself. 'You may go, Ms Jameson. I will send for you when I am ready.'

'But—'

Isobel started to speak, but one look at Alejandro's dark face and she thought better of it.

'Very well,' she said tightly, wishing she didn't feel so helpless. She would ring Uncle Sam, she decided firmly. No interview was worth what she being forced to endure.

CHAPTER NINE

ISOBEL spent the next half hour pacing about her sitting room, undecided as to what she ought to do.

Although the idea of ringing Sam had seemed fairly reasonable in the heat of the moment, now she wasn't so sure. Besides, she couldn't deny she was apprehensive about Alejandro's part in all of this. The last thing she needed was her uncle wading in in her defence and making things even worse.

If only she could be sure Alejandro had been lying when he'd said he could prove Emma was his daughter. And what if he hadn't? What then?

She had no idea how he'd found out about Emma in the first place. But instead of arguing with him—and the rest, she shivered—she should have behaved like the professional journalist she'd always believed herself to be and asked him.

He might not have answered her, of course. But at least she would have had the satisfaction of knowing she'd tried. The whole situation had changed so much since that first night when she'd arrived at the villa, when all she'd had to worry about was seeing Alejandro again. Now she had so much more to lose.

Someone knocked at her door and she stiffened. But it

wouldn't be Alejandro, she assured herself, impatient at the anxiety that just the thought of him could summon at will.

Still, she was relieved when she opened the door to Ricardo Vincente. Did this mean she was still employed? Or had Anita seen something in the hall that had made her change her mind?

'You will come with me, *senhora*,' Ricardo said with his usual air of officiousness. 'Senhora Silveira is ready for you.'

Isobel swallowed. 'Are you sure?' she ventured, ignoring the fact that she had gone in search of her hostess earlier.

'The *senhora* wishes to begin the interview immediately,' declared Ricardo a little impatiently. 'Come. I will show you to her apartments.'

As she crossed the hall again, Isobel saw that the maids had resumed their polishing. How discreet, she thought, not without a trace of bitterness. Did everybody dance to Alejandro's tune?

They took the stairs this time, ascending to a galleried landing that overlooked the hall below. Here, angled windows cast light on heavily patterned carpets, bronze urns and marbled statuary giving the corridor that led away from the landing an imposing ostentation.

At the end of the corridor, double doors signalled their destination. Ricardo tapped once, and after evidently hearing some response he flung the doors wide in a dramatic gesture.

'Ms Jameson, *senhora*,' he said, almost as if Anita was royalty. He gestured Isobel forward. '*Va em frente.* Go ahead.'

Isobel entered slowly, her eyes registering that this was not the office she'd expected. Slatted blinds at the windows revealed a spacious sitting-room, overstuffed sofas and chairs forming various seating arrangements about the floor.

A large square-patterned rug covered most of the area. An ornate stone-fireplace occupied a prominent position, faced by a tapestry screen. There were austere portraits on the antique-finished walls, and more of the self-conscious bric-a-brac decorating every available surface.

Anita was seated on a *chaise longue* in the window embrasure. And, just like her son-in-law downstairs, she'd positioned herself so her face was obscured by the brightness behind her. But as Isobel came in she rose to greet her, and the younger woman realised Anita was still wearing the filmy garments she'd been wearing earlier.

'Ms Jameson,' she said, her expression enigmatic. 'Do sit down, will you not? Ricardo, ask Sancha to arrange for some coffee.'

'*Sim, senhora.*'

Ricardo bowed and withdrew, and Isobel glanced a little nervously about her. 'Where would you like me to sit, *senhora*?' she asked, aware that her palms were sweating. And, because she was half-afraid she might drop her briefcase, she gathered it rather protectively against her chest.

Anita regarded her for a long, disturbing moment, and then she indicated the chair set at right angles to the *chaise*. 'Here, I think,' she said with a thin-lipped smile. Then, nodding towards the bag Isobel was clutching so protectively, 'You will not need that today, *senhora*. I hope you agree we need to get to know one another first, *nao e*?'

Isobel hesitated. 'Oh, but—'

'You have some objection, *senhora*?'

Anita arched imperious brows and Isobel realised she didn't have any choice if she wanted to do what she'd actually come here for. 'No. No,' she said putting down her briefcase and subsiding onto the chair Anita had suggested. 'But I'm not very interesting, Senhora Silveira. I'd really rather talk about you.'

Anita seated herself on the *chaise* again, stretching out her legs and spreading the folds of chiffon about her. Then, regarding her guest with an intensity Isobel found unnerving, she said, 'My son-in-law tells me you met in London some years ago.'

It was a daunting opening, and Isobel was taken aback. What, exactly, had Alejandro said? But, 'Yes,' she murmured, concentrating on a huge bee that was buzzing against the window. Then, 'You have a wonderful view, *senhora*. I imagine you find staying here much different from your home in Rio.'

'Why did you not mention it when I introduced you?' Anita was not to be diverted.

'Oh. Well, it was difficult,' said Isobel at last. Then, finding inspiration, 'I didn't want you to think I'd only come here because I knew Senhor Cabral.'

'And you had not?' Anita's brows arched again.

'Heavens, no.' At least on that score Isobel could be totally honest. 'He—' She cleared her throat. 'He was the last person I expected to see.'

'Mmm.'

Anita was obviously absorbing this, but Isobel didn't fool herself that that was to be an end to the matter. And she wasn't disappointed.

'And was this a business meeting?' Anita asked after a moment. 'Perhaps Cabral Leisure wanted to advertise in one of your uncle's magazines, yes?'

It was a temptation to agree, but Isobel suspected it was a trap, and decided to be as honest as she could be. 'It was at a birthday party, actually,' she said, trying to make light of it. 'A friend of mine, who is in the advertising industry, invited your son-in-law to come along. And—and he did.'

'And this was when?'

'Oh…' How to answer that? 'A few years ago,' she said at last. 'I can't actually give you a date.'

Although she could, to the exact day and time.

'And you haven't seen him since?'

'Not since he left London, no.'

Anita was silent for a few moments, and Isobel waited apprehensively for her to ask her to explain that statement.

But she didn't.

As if she'd decided she could save any further questions about Alejandro for another day, Anita lifted her arms above her head and stretched luxuriously.

Then, with the arrival of the maid with the coffee she'd ordered, she turned to less personal matters. She asked Isobel about her aunt and uncle, showing some interest in the fact that her aunt bred horses. For a moment, Isobel was sure she was going to mention Alejandro again.

But no. She went on to question Isobel about her work and her professional background, showing a polite interest in her answers, if nothing else.

However, by the time the coffee was finished, she was evidently getting bored. 'I am tired, *senhora*,' she said. 'We will continue our discussions tomorrow afternoon, *sim*? For now, you might like to rest also. Ricardo may have told you, I often work late into the night. That is why I am usually unavailable in the mornings.' Her lips twitched. 'I am sure you can find your own way back to your apartments.'

Alejandro half-expected Isobel to defy him.

When he arrived at the Villa Mimosa the following morning, he was quite prepared to have to force her to go with him. And force her he would, if he had to, he told himself. He had been looking forward to this day for far too long.

But, in the event, she was waiting for him on the veranda at the front of the villa. Although it was still quite early, she was neatly dressed in a plain V-necked olive tee-shirt and khaki shorts. Her hair, longer now than he remembered it, was braided into a thick plait that lay confidingly over her shoulder. She wore no jewellery and little make-up, but she still managed to look distractingly feminine.

Alejandro brought the Lexus to a halt at the foot of the shallow steps that led up to the veranda, and before he could open his door and get out Isobel had run down to join him.

Pulling open the opposite door, she said, 'Don't bother to get out. I can manage.' She swung herself up into the seat beside him with an agility that exposed slim thighs, lightly reddened by the sun. 'Okay.'

Alejandro regarded her quizzically. 'Forgive me,' he said, 'but I had not expected you to be so eager to spend the morning with me.'

'I'm not,' retorted Isobel flatly, even though his nearness made her pulses race. 'But as you seem to have difficulty walking….'

Alejandro's jaw tightened. 'You feel sorry for me, is that it?' He gave a harsh laugh. 'Please. I do not need your pity. And I am perfectly capable of getting in and out of this vehicle.'

Isobel cast him a frustrated look. If only he knew, she thought irritably. Far from feeling sorry for him, all her energies in that direction were concentrated on herself.

Didn't he realise that the scar on his cheek created an almost primitive fascination? That he had a raw sexuality that no amount of soul-searching on her part could totally dismiss? He wasn't the man she'd known in London, no, but he was far more dangerous. He was Emma's father, a fact that she'd conveniently managed to suppress until she'd come here.

'You've obviously injured your leg,' she said at last as he put the Lexus into gear. 'I was merely being considerate.'

'*Realmente?*'

'Yes, really,' she replied tersely. 'I'd do the same for anyone in your situation.'

'Tell it as it is, why do you not?' murmured Alejandro drily, and saw the way her full lips compressed into an impatient line.

But he really didn't want to waste the morning arguing with her. Or to arouse her enmity, if he hadn't done so already. His daughter was more important than that, more important than any resentment he might feel towards her. *Que droga*, but he was resentful. He'd missed out on the first two years of Emma's life.

Emma...

They drove through the small town of Porto Verde. Isobel, who hadn't left the villa except to go down to the beach since her arrival, looked about her with interest.

Like the village that was nearer the villa, Porto Verde reminded her of places she'd visited in the Caribbean. Square plots surrounded colour-washed houses whose tiled roofs steamed lightly in the morning sun. Even at this hour washing hung from haphazardly slung lines; dogs roamed at will, and children with huge brown eyes turned to watch them as they drove past.

She saw the airport in the distance, but Alejandro turned off the coast road and drove inland up a steeply climbing track. And away from the coast all signs of habitation disappeared, the road given over to hedges of flowering hibiscus and long grasses moving languidly in the barely perceptible breeze.

It was primitive, but beautiful. Much like the man she was with, she thought fancifully, still not entirely sure she was doing the right thing by coming with him. But what choice did she have, actually? She had to know what he knew about her and Emma.

She expelled a breath, feeling the heat outside pressing against the car's windows. Or was it just her temperature that was rising, driven by the tension inside the car?

'It's very beautiful,' she said at last, deciding to avoid any controversial questions for the moment. 'How far is it to—what was it you called it?—Montevideo?'

'Montevideo is in Uruguay,' said Alejandro flatly. 'The *estancia* is called Montevista. It is actually a Spanish name. It means—'

'Mountain view,' inserted Isobel with a grimace. 'I do understand a little simple Spanish, Alejandro.'

'Ah.'

Alejandro caught his breath, his fingers tightening about the wheel. He'd forgotten how good his name sounded on her tongue. Had forgotten a lot of things about her, he conceded ruefully. Most particularly, how easy it would be to let what happened the day before blind him to the real reason she was here.

All the same, he couldn't ignore the fact that he'd spent much of the night stressing over his own stupidity. Grabbing her like that, kissing her! *Por amor de Deus*, what had he been hoping to achieve?

To make love with her—that was the answer, he acknowledged grimly. For a few moments, he hadn't been able to think of anything else. And despite the passage of years he remembered everything about her. Which should have warned him how unpredictable bringing her to the *estancia* today was.

The sky overhead was a translucent blue. Isobel's eyes followed the vapour trail of a jet flying high above them, and caught a glimpse of a sinuous body before it disappeared into the grasses at the side of the track. A snake, perhaps? she wondered, recalling the warning her uncle had given her about the wildlife in this area. She shivered. Not all the creatures were friendly. And she wasn't only referring to the animals.

They eventually reached a sort of plateau and Isobel was grateful when the road straightened out. It had twisted and turned for miles, it seemed, and although she was normally a fairly good traveller her nerves weren't helping her roiling stomach.

The air was so clear, she saw, looking about her, realising that the blue line on the horizon was the sea. In the other direction purple mountains, half-shrouded in mist, looked distant and mysterious. Here, a heat haze hovered over miles of open grassland, the vast landscape punctuated by stands of pine or flowering acacia.

There were groups of cattle too, seeking shade beneath the trees. Rather dangerous-looking cattle, Isobel thought, their long, pointed horns turning irresistibly in their direction.

She was so busy taking it all in that she almost missed the stone gateposts with their arching logo of rearing stallions. The track narrowed between white-railed fences, steadily rising towards a sprawling mass of buildings about half a mile away.

There were more cattle here, and Isobel looked at Alejandro enquiringly. 'I thought this was a horse farm,' she said, gesturing towards the animals. 'Do you breed cattle too?'

'We try to be—what would you say?—sufficient, *nao*?' His smile was faintly mocking. 'Carlos, my manager, would consider any waste of *precioso*—um, valuable grazing land—a crime.'

They were approaching what appeared to be a small settlement now, and Isobel waited in unwilling anticipation for her first sight of Alejandro's house.

And, despite the number of outbuildings, the homestead itself was unmistakeable. The two-storeyed building had a wraparound veranda and dark-green shutters folded back from all the windows. Its walls were liberally covered with passion-flower vine, and there were numerous tubs of blossoms spilling their beauty in the shade of the first-floor balcony.

Isobel let out a breath she'd hardly known she was holding, and Alejandro cast a glance her way. 'Is something wrong?'

'Wrong?' Isobel shook her head. 'No. It's—it's lovely. I don't know; I thought it would be a little less—less—'

'Civilised?' suggested Alejandro drily, bringing the car to a halt on the gravelled forecourt, and she bit her lip.

'Sophisticated,' she amended, pushing open her door without thinking what she was doing, only to gasp for air as the unexpected altitude took her breath.

'Be careful,' said Alejandro, pushing open his own door and getting out rather less enthusiastically. 'We are several-hundred feet above sea level, but it is still very hot.'

'Tell me about it,' murmured Isobel, pushing out her lips and blowing air up over her hot face. She licked her dry lips. Then, pushing back the damp tendrils of hair that were clinging to her forehead, 'Do you ever get used to the heat?'

'In time,' said Alejandro, seemingly unmoved by the temperature, which even here had to be in the high eighties. 'Come. We will get some refreshment inside.'

Despite her reluctance to be alone with him, Isobel rounded the car to join him just as another man, a little older than Alejandro, appeared from the back of the house.

'Ah,' he said, coming to greet Alejandro with a smile on his face. *'O que voce esta fazendo?'* His eyes turned to Isobel. *'Quem isto e?'*

'Ingles, por favor, Carlos,' said Alejandro wryly. 'This is Ms Jameson. The young woman I was telling you about.'

'Ah, Mees Jameson.'

Carlos's accent was more pronounced than Alejandro's, but his smile was infinitely more friendly. He held out his hand towards her. 'Carlos Ferreira, *senhorita*. I am happy to meet you.'

'Isobel,' said Isobel at once, shaking his hand a little too enthusiastically. But it was a relief to know they weren't alone after all. 'I understand you do all the work around here.'

Carlos laughed then, white teeth showing below the rim of his dark moustache. 'I cannot believe this man said that,' he said, clapping his friend on the shoulder. 'But if you would like a—how do you say?—a tour of the stables, *nao*? I am your man.'

Isobel glanced at Alejandro, but his expression was unreadable. With a little shrug, she said, 'I'd like that very much.'

'But not now, *sim*?' suggested Alejandro, his quiet voice as commanding as an order. He smiled at Carlos as if to soften his words. 'Ms—*Isobella*—is hot and thirsty. I will ask Consuela if she has something cold and sweet.'

Isobel started to protest, but, after exchanging a few brief words with Alejandro in their own language, Carlos turned way.

'Until later, Isobella,' he called, raising his hand in

farewell, and Isobel had no choice but to accompany Alejandro across the veranda and through the open doors into the house.

CHAPTER TEN

BEYOND the entry, the wood-blocked floor of a reception hall echoed with the sound of their feet. Shafts of sunlight fell through a series of narrow windows, and the air was sweet with the scent of verbena.

It was very different from the gloomy magnificence of Anita's villa. Here, colour-washed walls and a beamed ceiling gave the place a much more lived-in appearance. There were paintings on the walls, and a huge central table fairly spilling with vibrant colour. An enormous bowl of tropical flowers formed a brilliant centrepiece, while exotic stems of orchids grew from various pots and planters about the room.

A woman came to meet them as they crossed the hall, a small, dark-skinned woman, dressed all in black, but with pleasant, friendly features. Much different from Sancha, thought Isobel with relief, remembering Anita's housekeeper's unsmiling demeanour.

'This is Elena,' said Alejandro at once, smiling at the woman. 'Elena, this is Ms Jameson. A—friend of mine.'

Isobel was fairly sure his hesitation had been deliberate, but Elena didn't seem to notice. *'Bemvindo da quinta, senhora,'* she said, bobbing her head politely. Then, turning back to Alejandro, *'Voce gostaria um cafe, senhor?'*

Isobel's simple grasp of Portuguese was enough to know that the woman had welcomed her to the *estancia*. And she wasn't absolutely sure, but she thought she'd also asked if they'd like coffee.

'Fruit juice, I think, Elena,' responded Alejandro, proving she'd been right. He glanced at Isobel. 'And some iced tea also, *sim*? We will be in the *conservatorio*.'

'Sim, senhor.'

With another bob of her head, Elena departed and Alejandro turned once more to his guest. 'Come,' he said. 'I will show you a little of my house.'

Isobel shrugged, aware that she didn't have a lot of choice in the matter, but she was curious nonetheless. This place was so different from the Villa Mimosa. And not just its appearance. The atmosphere was different too.

An open-plan living space led from the hall into a spacious salon with an Italian-tiled floor. The coffered ceiling was supported by veined marble pillars, dividing the room into elegant seating areas with the huge stone-faced hearth as a backdrop.

Isobel couldn't help moving forward to where long windows overlooked an outdoor patio. Wickerwork chairs were grouped around a glass-topped table, shaded again by the balcony above. And, beyond the patio, a pool sparkled invitingly in the sunlight, with woven, wooden *cabanas* where Alejandro's guests could change their clothes.

Isobel's tongue sought her upper lip. She'd never imagined anything like this. Villiers, her aunt and uncle's home, was beautiful, but she knew already it didn't compare with Montevista.

She couldn't prevent a sudden intake of breath, and at once Alejandro came to join her. He walked a little stiffly, but it didn't appear to impede his progress this morning, his tawny eyes assessing her with wary intent.

'You do not like this place?'

Isobel gave him an old-fashioned look. 'How could I not?' she asked drily. 'It's very beautiful, and I'm sure you know it.' She paused. 'Did you buy it when you were married to Miranda?'

Alejandro's lips compressed. 'And why would you think that?'

'Oh, I don't know.' Isobel shrugged, very conscious of him standing close beside her. 'I just thought Senhora Silveira might have told you about it. After all, it's in the same general area.'

Alejandro expelled a breath. 'Montevista has been in my family for generations,' he told her at last. 'My great-grandfather built it so that my great-grandmother could use it as an escape from the city. There was no air-conditioning in those days and, although it does not seem so at this moment, the mountain air is fresher. It can be cold, too, believe it or not. We have to light the fire from time to time.'

Isobel absorbed this. 'So you don't actually own it?'

'No.' Alejandro spoke tolerantly, rubbing an impatient hand over his aching thigh. 'It just so happens that, well, let us say it is a good place to—recuperate, *nao*? And I have always loved horses. I sometimes think I would rather be a *cavaleiro*—a horseman—than spend my days in an office.'

Isobel glanced at him then, noticing that he was favouring his injured leg. 'You had to recuperate,' she said slowly, aware of a certain sympathy. 'After the accident. Is that right?'

Alejandro's lips twisted. 'As you say.' He turned then, gesturing that she should precede him through an archway into an adjoining salon, where a formal polished table and a dozen upholstered chairs occupied a central position. 'The conservatory,' he added unnecessarily, indicating a huge glass-walled extension beyond sliding-glass doors.

Despite its many windows, the conservatory was kept to an even temperature by air-conditioning and the use of half-drawn blinds. Tubs containing shrubs and climbing plants added their own particular fragrance to the air, and comfortable chairs and cushioned loungers provided plenty of seating space.

'If you don't mind…'

Without waiting for her permission, Alejandro lowered himself onto one of the loungers, stretching out his aching leg with real relief. He was overdoing things, he knew, but it still annoyed him to show her any weakness. Her opinion of him mattered, however ridiculous that might be.

'Oh, of course.' Isobel swung round from her examination of an orange tree, the small, immature fruits so amazing in their natural habitat. 'Um…' She chose a chair some distance away from him and massaged its arms with nervous fingers. 'Is your leg painful? I saw you rubbing it before.'

'It has been better,' said Alejandro tightly, not wanting to get into a discussion about his shortcomings. 'Ah, at last. Here is Elena. If you would put the tray beside Ms Jameson, Elena, *por favor.*'

Elena evidently understood a little English, because she did as Alejandro had asked, and then straightened with an enquiring smile.

'*O almoço, senhor?*' she said. And then, as if interpreting the look he gave her, she amended it to, 'Lunch, *senhor*? You like for two?'

'*Receio que nao*, Elena. I am afraid not,' Alejandro answered her politely. 'Ms Jameson has to return to Porto Verde.' He paused, his eyes flickering over Isobel's flushed face. 'Another day, perhaps.'

'*Sim, senhor.*'

Elena bowed again and left them, her rubber-soled shoes making little sound on the tiled floor. Isobel turned her attention to the tray the woman had placed on the low table beside her.

Chilled fruit juice stood in a frosted jug, iced tea clinking in a tall container. There were chilled glasses too, misting in the warmer air of the conservatory, and a bowl of ice melting in the heat.

'Um, what would you like?' she asked, guessing Alejandro had had the tray placed near her deliberately, but he shook his head.

'Nothing for me,' he said. 'But help yourself to whatever you prefer.'

Isobel picked up the jug of fruit juice, managing to half-fill a glass without her shaking hand depositing most of it on the tray. She added a handful of ice cubes and then raised the glass to her lips, trying not to feel self-conscious, because his hooded eyes never left her face.

It was delicious, a mixture of pear, pomegranate and passion fruit, she thought. Whatever, it was just what she needed to give some moisture to her dry throat, and not even Alejandro's scrutiny could totally spoil her enjoyment.

'So,' he said, when it was obvious she wasn't about to say anything. 'Is it good?'

'Very good,' said Isobel hurriedly, wiping a dribble of juice from her chin. 'Thank you. It's delicious.'

'Good.' Alejandro adjusted the back of his seat so he could relax more comfortably and then said, 'Why are you afraid of me?'

'I'm not afraid.' Isobel put down her glass rather abruptly. 'Apprehensive, perhaps,' she added. 'I'd like to know what all this is about.'

'All what?' enquired Alejandro carelessly. 'Coming here? Enjoying a glass of fruit juice? What?'

'You know what I mean,' said Isobel tersely, unable to sit still under his mocking interrogation. She paced rapidly about the conservatory, pushing aside trailing ferns that caught her hair as she passed. 'Why you've brought me here. What you intend to do about Emma. I don't understand why you want to disrupt my life. I've done nothing to hurt you.'

'You think?' Alejandro's mouth compressed now, and despite her agitation Isobel was struck by the savage beauty his face possessed. It had been ravaged by his scar, but that wasn't important. It had lost little of its masculine appeal.

Alejandro sat up then and leant towards her. 'Why do you not come and sit?' he suggested mildly. 'You are making yourself hot and uncomfortable pacing about the floor.' But when she reluctantly turned back towards her chair, he gestured impatiently. 'Not there,' he said, indicating the chair beside him. 'Keeping your distance from me is not going to change the situation.'

Isobel blew out a frustrated breath, but she felt compelled to do as he said. Besides, she told herself, she wasn't afraid of him—only that her unwilling attraction to him might make her vulnerable.

'All right,' she said, trying to sound confident. 'Why did you say you had proof that Emma is your daughter?'

Alejandro regarded her narrowly. 'Because I do.'

'I don't believe you.'

'No? Believe it or not, I had gathered that,' said Alejandro drily. Shifting in his seat, he pulled a wallet out of his back pocket and flicked it open. And as he did so, a small photograph dropped onto the seat of the lounger beside him.

The photograph fell face-up and Isobel's eyes were drawn to it at once. Dear God, she thought, he had a picture of Emma. Had he been following her? How else could he have got something like this?

Snatching up the picture with trembling fingers, she thrust it towards him, her eyes riveted on his dark face. 'What do you think you're doing?' she demanded. 'Don't you know it's an offence to stalk people, particularly children? How have you got a picture of my daughter?'

Alejandro regarded her with faint amusement. 'It is not a picture of your daughter,' he said mildly. 'What you are holding is a picture of my niece, Caterina.'

'What?'

Isobel pulled her hand down again and stared at the picture with disbelieving eyes.

The smiling face that looked back at her was amazingly like Emma's: dancing eyes, baby-soft cheeks, dimples, and a generous mouth. But, although the child's hair was the same colour as Emma's, it was much longer, glossy ringlets framing the small face.

Isobel caught her breath.

He was right. It wasn't Emma. If she'd paid more attention to the picture before jumping in with both feet, she'd have noticed this. And the fact that Emma didn't have the kind of dress Caterina was wearing.

Indeed, Emma was a tomboy. She could usually be found in dungarees and a tee-shirt, small boots on her feet as she helped Aunt Olivia clean out the horses' stalls.

Of course, she wore a dress sometimes. But nothing as elaborate as this. If Isobel wasn't mistaken, Caterina's dress was silk. Not the kind of thing she would dress her daughter in at all.

She looked up and found Alejandro was still watching her. With burning cheeks, she said, 'All right. It's not a picture of Emma. I was mistaken.' She paused. 'But don't pretend you didn't do that on purpose.'

'Do what on purpose?'

He was all innocence, and Isobel was infuriated.

'Drop the picture so I would see it,' she retorted, thrusting it onto the arm of his chair. 'You're not a clumsy man, Alejandro. You wanted me to see it. You wanted me to jump to the obvious conclusion.'

'Was it obvious?' Alejandro regarded her for another long, disturbing moment. Then he picked up the small photograph and slotted it back into his wallet. '*Contudo,*' he added. 'Nevertheless, I think it proves my point, do you not think so?'

Isobel blew out a weary breath. 'Okay, okay,' she said, deciding there was nothing to be gained from arguing with him. 'You are Emma's father.' Her nails dug into her palms. 'Does it matter?'

'You ask me that?' Alejandro's voice was harsh with anger now. '*Meu Deus*, Isobel, did you not think I had a right to know?'

'To know what?' Isobel was trembling, but she refused to be intimidated. 'That you'd accidently impregnated a woman you had sex with while you were in London?'

Alejandro swore now. 'It was not like that and you know it.'

'What was it like, then? You tell me.' Isobel was on a roll now and she wasn't ready to back down. 'You seduced me, Alejandro. Oh, I admit, I didn't put up much opposition. I was reckless, I know that. But don't pretend it was some lasting affair and you were the innocent party.'

Alejandro scowled. 'You do not know what you are talking about.'

'Oh, I do.' Isobel got to her feet again, gazing down at him with accusing eyes. 'Don't you remember what you said, Alejandro? You promised you'd come back to England. You insisted it wasn't just a one-night stand. But—hello—it's been over three years, and until you brought me here I hadn't heard a word from you.'

'I can explain.'

'Can you?' Isobel didn't want to hear his excuses, didn't want to hear anything that might make her regret her outburst. 'I actually believed you, Alejandro. I did think I'd see you again. But now I find that you got married as soon as you got back to Brazil.'

'Not as soon as I got back to Brazil,' Alejandro contradicted her harshly, pushing himself to his feet now so that he had the height advantage, not her. 'When I said you did not know what you were talking about, I meant the accident. While you were hating my guts, no doubt, I was in the hospital in Rio, in no fit state to contact you or anyone else.'

Isobel took a deep breath. So, she thought, he had an excuse after all. There was nothing she could say now that could counter that.

Still, she consoled herself defensively, it wasn't her fault he'd had an accident. And he'd had plenty of time since then to get in touch with her. Just because he'd suddenly—what? Remembered her? Got a conscience? Why had he sought her out after all this time?

Backing up a bit, not wanting him to suspect how his nearness affected her, Isobel lifted her shoulders in a dismissive gesture. 'So—I'm sorry. But I don't see what you expect me to do now.'

Alejandro uttered a disbelieving oath. 'You do not see?' he echoed hoarsely, taking a step towards her. 'You think that by admitting Emma is my daughter you have absolved yourself of all responsibility for what happens in the future?'

'No.' Isobel forced herself not to back away again. 'But you can't pretend that you feel something for a child you've never even seen!'

'Oh, I have seen her,' retorted Alejandro, his hot breath lifting the hair against her forehead, and Isobel gasped.

'You came to England?'

'Not to see her, no,' Alejandro said, admitting he had been in London. He remembered how poignant his memories of the city and Isobel had seemed at that time. He sighed now. 'But the Internet is a wonderful thing. And photographs transfer so well.'

Isobel gazed up at him, aghast. 'But you said—'

'*Sim?* What did I say?'

'You let me think you didn't have any pictures of Emma.'

'Did I do that?'

'You know you did.' Isobel struggled to sort her confused thoughts into some semblance of order. 'Are you telling me you have been stalking me after all?'

Alejandro groaned. He'd been afraid she might see it like this. 'For your information, the Cabral company employs a firm of trouble-shooters to police our European operation. They work out of the London office, and I asked one of them—a friend of mine called Andrew Hardy—to check up on you.'

Isobel gasped. 'I don't believe it. Why would you do a thing like that?'

Alejandro shrugged now. 'Why not?' His lips twisted as he remembered the heart-searching he'd indulged in before giving Andrew the go-ahead. 'Perhaps I was curious about you. After all, we did share something which I, at least, considered worthy of revisiting.'

'Don't.' Isobel stepped back from him now and he saw the look of contempt in her eyes. 'Don't pretend you ever cared about me.' She shook her head. 'Alejandro, you married someone else. After we had been together. Please don't insult my intelligence by pretending our relationship meant anything to you. Not then and not now.'

Alejandro's jaw tightened. 'Not now, I agree,' he said bitterly, and Isobel caught her breath. 'I am not a complete fool.'

'What's that supposed to mean?'

'I think you know, *cara*.' His tone was scornful. 'I see the way you look at me, the way you back off every time I invade your space.'

'That's not true!' Isobel couldn't let him go on thinking such a thing. 'It's just—it's just—'

She stumbled to a halt, incapable of voicing something she was unwilling to admit even to herself.

How could she tell him what she was really feeling? Trapped in the emotion of the moment, it would be so easy to destroy the promises she'd made to herself, to put not just her own but Emma's future at risk.

'You see?' he said harshly, totally misunderstanding her hesitation. 'I knew it yesterday morning when I held you in my arms. You can deny it if you wish, but you cannot deny that as soon as I let you go you could not wait to get away.'

'Senhora Silveira was there,' protested Isobel, but Alejandro was unconvinced.

'So?' he mocked. 'I do not repulse you, *querida*?'

'Of course not!'

'Of course not!' He mimicked her words, dragging the heel of his hand over the diagonal ridge that scarred his face. 'You are attracted to a man such as me?' And, when he saw her shaking her head, he muttered grimly. 'I thought not.'

'You don't understand.'

'I understand only too well,' he said, crowding her against the vine-covered trellis behind her, and it took every scrap of determination Isobel had to stand her ground.

'Alejandro.'

But, before she could say any more, she was silenced by the savage pressure of his mouth covering hers.

There was no tenderness in his kiss. He didn't hold her with any of the warmth and sensitivity he'd shown the previous day. Indeed, he made no attempt to hold her at all, though the hard strength of his body enveloped her in his heat.

The kiss was intended to punish her, and when he forced her lips to part she tasted blood on her tongue. He couldn't fail to taste it too, she thought, and the muffled oath he uttered seemed to confirm this.

Yet it didn't halt his fierce assault or the hungry possession of his mouth. With every thrust of his tongue, he was proving that he wanted her, and she was fairly sure that hadn't been his intention at all.

'Raios o partam!' he groaned. 'Damn you!' He spoke against her lips, and her lungs inhaled his breath, his scent. Then almost angrily he reached for her, gripping her hips and forcing her into even closer contact with his aroused body.

'I want you,' he said roughly. 'I want to be inside you.' He drew back to look down at her, his expression harsh with loathing. 'And how crazy is that?'

'Alejandro…'

But someone was coming, with heavier footsteps than the maid who had brought the tray of fruit juice. Alejandro turned to face the newcomer with what he told himself was a feeling of relief.

'Carlos,' he said tightly as the older man appeared in the doorway. 'You are just in time. I think our guest is ready for your tour.'

CHAPTER ELEVEN

'You enjoyed your outing to Alex's *estancia*?'

It was the following afternoon. Despite the fact that Isobel had returned to the Villa Mimosa in plenty of time to spend the previous afternoon with Anita, the older woman had not been available.

According to Ricardo, she'd been suffering another of her migraines. But Isobel couldn't help wondering if the frequency of these attacks was due more to her presence than to any innate weakness on Anita's part.

Now, with Anita watching her with shrewd, assessing eyes, Isobel felt the colour flooding into her throat and rising irresistibly into her face. 'Um, yes, *senhora*. Very much,' she said uneasily, wondering whether Alejandro had spoken to his mother-in-law since her return. Carlos had brought her back to the villa, but Alejandro could have phoned.

Or visited, come to that. How would she have known?

'You did not think it was a little remote, being so far from the city?' Anita persisted.

'I—no.' Isobel didn't know what Anita was getting at. 'I just thought it was very beautiful.'

Anita clicked her tongue impatiently. 'You use that word a lot, do you not, Ms Jameson? You think my home is—' she made quotation marks with her fingers '—beautiful, or so you said. And now you think Alex's *estancia* is—' once again she snapped her fingers together '—beautiful also.' She snorted. 'I trust this article you are hoping to write will not be filled with euphemisms too.'

'They're not euphemisms, *senhora*.' Isobel was defensive.

'No?' Anita was sceptical. 'Perhaps you say what you think your listener wants to hear?' Her eyes narrowed. 'How well did you and Alex know one another when he was in London? Tell me, did you only come here to see him?'

Isobel was shocked at the change of topic. 'No,' she said unsteadily. 'Of course not.'

'Perhaps you have changed your mind since you got here?' Anita suggested coldly. 'The Alex you knew in London must have been much different from the man you see today.'

Isobel caught her breath. 'I had no idea Alejandro was your son-in-law,' she protested, wondering what he had said to arouse such a response.

'But that does not really answer my question, does it, *senhora*?' Anita retorted sharply. 'Does his appearance offend you? You were evidently unaware he had had an accident or that his injuries were so acute.'

Isobel shook her head. 'Really, *senhora*, I'd prefer it if we concentrated on less personal matters.'

'So why are you trying to insinuate yourself into this family?'

'I'm not—'

'I would have thought that, as a mother yourself, you would have been eager to get back to your little girl.'

'I am.'

'How old is your daughter, Ms Jameson? She cannot be much more than a baby. Am I not right?'

Isobel stiffened. 'Why do you say that?' she asked, without giving herself time to think it through.

Anita's lips thinned. 'Why, because as far as I am aware, you were not married when my son-in-law first knew you, Ms Jameson. *Portanto*, therefore, that was only—*que?*—three years ago, *nao*?'

Isobel expelled an uneven breath. 'Emma's nearly three,' she said, not altogether truthfully. 'Now.' She paused. 'Do you think we could return to the matter in hand?'

'But this is the matter in hand,' Anita contradicted her pleasantly. 'I want to know all about you, Ms Jameson. Before I bare my soul to you, I need to be sure you are— how shall I say?—sympathetic, *nao*?'

Isobel straightened her spine. They were sitting in the library today, where Ricardo had told her Anita did most of her work. A large room, with walls lined with leather-bound volumes, it was a little oppressive, like the rest of the house.

There was a square mahogany desk in the middle of the floor, and Anita was seated in the leather chair behind it. Isobel had been confined to a stiff-backed dining chair, intended to put her in her place, she was sure.

'I'm sure my life hasn't been half as eventful as yours, *senhora*,' she said now, hoping to distract the woman. 'Can we talk about your first book? I've read that you wrote it while you were recovering from the birth of your daughter, Miranda.'

'Actually, the birth you are referring to was of my son, Miguel,' retorted Anita shortly. 'He died when he was only a few weeks old. I was recovering from his death, not Miranda's birth.'

'Oh.' Isobel hadn't known that. Indeed, in all the publicity she'd read about Anita, there'd been no mention of a son.

But it might explain the tone of the book, which was distinctly sombre. 'I apologise, *senhora*. I had no wish to intrude.'

'But is that not what you are doing?' asked Anita, arching dark brows interrogatively.

'Only as far as your books are concerned,' Isobel assured her firmly. She was sure Sam was expecting some personal details too, but she had no intention of writing an exposé.

She bit her lip. 'Returning to your first book, *senhora*—is the hero of the story based on anyone in history? It has been suggested that you've used Shakespeare's interpretation of Richard the Third as a source for your character, Alonzo.'

'When did you get married, Ms Jameson?'

Once again, Isobel was taken aback. But clearly Anita had no intention of continuing with the interview until she was satisfied with Isobel's answers.

'Um, when I was twenty-one,' she replied truthfully, and then realised that wasn't the answer Anita had been looking for.

'Twenty-one?' she echoed in some surprise. 'So you *were* married when you met Alex.' Her lips pursed consideringly. 'Does he know this?'

Isobel sighed. 'I was divorced two years later,' she said resignedly. 'My marriage to David was not a success. As a matter of fact, he was killed in an earthquake in Indonesia just a year after we separated.'

'But you married again?' Anita insisted. 'Emma cannot be your late husband's child.'

'No.' Isobel didn't know where this was leading, but she didn't like it. 'I've been single for about six years.'

'Ah.' Anita's tongue circled her lips as if in satisfaction. 'So your daughter is illegitimate, is she not?'

Isobel gasped. She could hardly speak, she was so angry. 'I think that's my business, *senhora*,' she got out at last. 'And, if you're going to waste time discussing my private life, I think we should abandon the interview, don't you?'

'Oh, Ms Jameson!' Anita's expression was contrite now. 'I did not mean to offend you.' Although Isobel was sure she had. 'Forgive me, *senhora*. I am a writer, and naturally I am interested in the lives of everyone I come into contact with.' Her smile was penitent. 'Please do not upset yourself. How you choose to live your life is your concern, of course.'

Yes, it is, thought Isobel furiously.

She badly wanted to walk out then. Despite Anita's facile plea for forgiveness, she didn't trust her an inch. But her uncle was depending on her, and she'd dealt with more awkward interviews. If only she knew what Alejandro's intentions might be...

Alejandro turned into the drive of the Villa Mimosa and parked the Lexus some distance from the house. He didn't want to encounter Anita unless he had to. It was Isobel—and Isobel alone—he'd come to see.

It was three days since he'd seen her, three days since he'd asked Carlos to drive her back to the villa. Three days, during part of which time he'd immersed himself in savage physical activity; anything to help him come to terms with the fact that his feelings for Isobel were not something he could control.

It was so frustrating.

He'd thought about her a lot over the years, though he doubted she would believe that. Particularly when he'd been lying in a hospital bed, having to accept the fact that he was never going to be the man he'd been before the accident.

By then, his injuries had no longer been life-threatening, but the torn ligaments in his thigh meant that he would never walk normally again. And the plastic surgeons had had to concede that even a series of operations would not save the right side of his face from being permanently scarred.

He'd been bitter then. He'd felt like a gargoyle, a monster; he'd felt sure no woman would look at him without either loathing or pity—and the idea of returning to London and laying himself open to Isobel's revulsion had not been on the cards.

Of course, over time, things had improved. He'd realised, with some amazement, that there were women who actually found his injuries appealing. They regarded him as some latter-day Prometheus, who'd fought off pain and injury and won through. Or perhaps, he'd decided in his more cynical moments, his fabulous wealth could overcome a multitude of sins.

And, through it all, there'd been Miranda: always there, always remorseful, blaming herself and eager to prove her loyalty in the way their families had always hoped for.

He scowled now, getting out of the car and closing the door as silently as possible. He winced as his weight bore down on his damaged leg. His efforts to avoid thinking about Isobel by riding out with the *vaqueiros* and roping steers had proved a more physical punishment than a mental one. She hadn't been out of his thoughts, not once, and he'd known he'd have to deal with the situation once and for all.

That was why he'd saved his visit until the evening when he could be sure of darkness to aid his objective. According to the manservant he'd bribed on Isobel's arrival, her rooms opened onto the veranda at the back of the villa, which was very convenient for his needs. Painful it might be, but he could get round to the back of the house without encountering any of the household staff.

It was after ten o'clock already, and he hoped Isobel wasn't in bed. He'd delayed his visit until this time just in case she had had dinner with Anita. Though, knowing his mother-in-law as he did, he doubted she would encourage such familiarity between them.

Anita hadn't phoned since the morning after Isobel's visit to the *estancia*, when she'd been trying to find out what had happened. He guessed she was still suspicious about their relationship, and he wondered how long it would be before she put two and two together and realised Isobel's child must be his.

Perhaps she'd already realised it, he conceded, stifling a groan as a particularly awkward bamboo-shoot dug into his hip as he squeezed past. But what of it? He had nothing to be ashamed of.

He breathed a sigh of relief when he reached the veranda and saw the lights still burning in Isobel's apartments. Dragging his leg, he made his way towards her door, and then stopped for a moment to regain his composure before raising his hand to knock.

There was complete silence for what seemed like a very long minute, and he was beginning to wonder if she was there after all when he heard footsteps.

'Who's there?' Isobel's voice sounded strained and anxious, and Alejandro leaned wearily against the wall beside the door.

'Me,' he said flatly. 'Alejandro.' He paused. 'Open the door.'

Once again, there was a short silence, and he was speculating on his ability to force the door open without causing too much noise or damage when the handle turned.

Isobel stood there, clad only in the cream cotton-vest and shorts he suspected she used to sleep in. Her face was flushed and defensive, but her expression changed when the light from inside the room fell on his face.

'My God!' she exclaimed. 'Are you ill?' She stepped forward without hesitation and took hold of his arm. 'Here, let me help you.'

Alejandro tried to throw off her hand. '*Obrigado*— thanks. I can manage,' he said harshly, but Isobel refused to give up.

'Don't be such a fool!' she exclaimed, assisting him over the threshold and into the lamplit room. 'How on earth did you get here? Did you walk?'

'Well, not from Montevista,' said Alejandro drily, feeling the sweat breaking out on his face. Gripping the back of a chair, he managed to straddle it, and sank down with some relief. 'I am okay,' he added as Isobel still hovered beside him. 'Close the door, hmm? I would prefer it if we did not have an audience.'

'Oh! Oh, yes.'

As if just realising the door was still standing wide, Isobel hurried to close it, turning the deadbolt almost automatically. Hopefully Anita was still working, she thought, but as far as the Brazilian woman was concerned she couldn't be sure of anything.

Alejandro folded his arms along the back of the chair and rested his chin on his wrists. Then, realising Isobel was still watching him with troubled eyes, he managed a faint smile.

'I will survive,' he assured her. 'I twisted my hip, that is all.' He blew out a breath. 'It feels better already.'

Isobel twisted her hands together at her waist. She wasn't wearing any make-up, and with her hair loose about her shoulders she looked absurdly young, he thought.

And far too desirable for his peace of mind.

Then, carefully, she said, 'How did you damage your leg?'

'I have just explained.'

'No. You know what I mean.' Isobel sighed. 'Was—was Miranda injured too?'

'Ah.' Alejandro lifted his head, relieved to feel the pain subsiding at last. 'You mean in the car crash. Do you think perhaps that was why she killed herself? Because, unlike me, she could not stand to look in a mirror, *nao*?'

'No!'

Isobel shifted her weight from one bare foot to the other. But that thought had entered her head and he knew it.

'For your information, Miranda was in the car when it crashed,' he told her briefly. 'But you will be happy to hear she walked away unscathed.'

'Oh.'

Alejandro regarded her through narrowed lids. 'Is that all you can say—oh?' His lips twisted. 'Miranda's death had nothing to do with the accident.'

'That's good.'

'Is it?' He sucked in a rueful breath. 'Yes, I suppose it is. At least no one blamed me.'

'Because you were driving when the accident occurred?'

Alejandro sighed. '*Escuta aqui*—look, can we talk about something else other than the accident? That is not why I came here. I understand only too well your feelings about my injuries.'

Isobel gasped. 'You don't know anything!' she exclaimed fiercely. She glanced towards the table where Alejandro now saw she had been working on her computer. There was a pot of coffee standing on a tray beside it, and she gestured towards it, saying, 'Why don't you have some coffee? I think it's still hot.'

'I think not, *cara*.' Alejandro's mouth turned down. 'And, if this is another attempt to distract me, forget it. You are wasting your time.'

'I'm not trying to distract you,' protested Isobel indignantly. 'But, well, in the circumstances it seemed the polite thing to do. I'm afraid I can't offer you anything stronger.'

'You think?'

Alejandro's tone was dry, but already his imagination was working overtime. She was obviously not aware that, without a bra, her tight little nipples were pressing against the thin cotton of her vest. His senses swam at the idea that she was also naked under those skimpy shorts.

He felt his instant arousal and forced himself to address the reason why he was really here. He knew that if he touched her he would not be able to stop.

'Why do you not sit down?' he suggested, knowing he'd feel happier if she wasn't standing over him.

'All right.' With a little gesture of indifference, Isobel perched on the edge of a squashy brocade-sofa, crossing her legs so that he was treated to a glimpse of her upper thigh. Then, as if it had just occurred to her, 'Does Senhora Silveira know you're here?'

'*Nao.*' Alejandro spoke abruptly. 'I did not come here to see Anita.'

'I see.' Isobel smoothed a moist palm over her bare knee. 'So…?'

'So.' Alejandro regarded her from between narrowed lids. 'Tell me about Emma.'

Isobel hesitated. 'What do you want to know?'

Alejandro stifled a groan. 'Do not try my patience, Isobella. I want to know everything. Have you brought any pictures of her with you?'

Isobel's breathing became a little difficult. 'Some,' she conceded reluctantly.

'Then may I see them?'

'Well, most of what I have are at home, of course.'

'I realise that.' Alejandro controlled his temper with an effort. 'Naturally I did not expect anything else. But, if I could see…?'

'All right.'

Isobel got to her feet and crossed to the table, where her phone was lying beside her coffee cup. Returning to her seat, she switched it on and quickly turned to the gallery of pictures she carried everywhere with her. Then, passing the phone to Alejandro, she said, 'There you are.'

Alejandro flicked slowly through the selection of photographs that were stored in the phone's memory, his reaction impossible for Isobel to read.

'And she is two years old, *sim*?'

'Two and a half,' Isobel corrected him tersely.

'She is very beautiful.'

Isobel's lips twitched with an unwilling smile. 'She's adorable,' she admitted. 'But don't be taken in by her appearance. She's a real tomboy.'

'A tomboy?' Alejandro frowned and he looked up. 'What is that?'

'Oh, she likes doing the things boys do,' said Isobel, unable to think of any other way to describe it. 'Getting dirty, for example. She's never happier than when she's down at the stables with Aunt Olivia.'

'*E claro.* Of course.' Alejandro nodded. 'Your aunt breeds horses too, does she not?'

'Not thoroughbreds,' said Isobel, remembering the almost pure-blooded horseflesh Carlos had shown her at Montevista. 'She rears Shetland ponies and hunters, mostly for riding schools or private use.'

Alejandro nodded. 'I look forward to meeting her.'

Isobel's jaw dropped. 'You're coming to England?'

'Does that bother you?'

'I—' Isobel was speechless. Then, gathering her wits, 'It doesn't bother me, but—'

'Well, I shall have to if I want to meet my daughter,' he continued, returning his attention to the pictures of Emma. Then, with a cynical smile, 'But not yet, eh, *pequena*? We do not want to frighten you, do we?'

Isobel stared at him. It would have been so easy to let his comment pass unnoticed, but she found she had far too much respect for him to do that.

'You wouldn't frighten her!' she exclaimed, though she could see he didn't believe her. 'Emma's not some delicate hothouse flower. She's bright and she's resilient. Besides, children don't look at things the way adults do.'

'The way you do?' suggested Alejandro bitterly, handing the phone back to her. Then, without waiting for her answer, he got heavily to his feet. 'We will talk again, Isobella. Be assured of it.'

Moving necessitated swinging his uninjured leg across the seat of the chair again. Alejandro tried to show the same restraint he'd exhibited on his arrival, but all the physical activity he'd put himself through during the day had left him stiff, and he staggered. Grabbing the back of the chair, he tried to right himself, but it was no good. The chair overturned and he found himself pitching forward, struggling to regain his balance.

Isobel saw what was happening, of course, and jumped automatically to her feet to try and save him. But she wasn't strong enough, and although Alejandro ordered her to get out of the way she didn't listen to him.

In consequence, the force of his body carried her

backward. She found herself spreadeagled on the sofa where she'd been sitting, with Alejandro's not-inconsiderable weight on top of her.

CHAPTER TWELVE

ALEJANDRO SWORE, forcing himself up immediately, his hands at either side of her head as he tried not to crush all the air out of her lungs.

'*Meu Deus! Perdao!* I'm sorry.' He pushed himself back, straddling her body, his knees hard against the bones of her hips. '*Que idiota!* What an idiot!'

'It doesn't matter.' Isobel spoke a little breathlessly, but a smile was tugging at the corners of her lips. 'Honestly, Alejandro, it was an accident, that's all. I shouldn't have interfered.'

'You were trying to help,' Alejandro contradicted her grimly, struggling to get his own breath back. Faint colour stained his cheeks at the ignominy of his position. '*Deus*, what must you think of me? Not only disfigured, but— what do you say?—decrepit as well.'

'You're not decrepit!'

Isobel gazed up at him impatiently. She wanted to reassure him, to tell him that she didn't think any the worse of him for proving he was human after all. And as for being disfigured...

Her hand moved almost of its own volition. Without hesitation, it reached up and stroked the ridge of scar tissue that crossed his cheek. He jerked back at once, but she persisted in her exploration, the skin at either side of the scar feeling as smooth as it ever had.

'*Nao,*' he said harshly, capturing her hand within his much larger one. 'Do not do that.'

'Why not?'

She spoke defiantly, and although she expected him to let her go now he brought her hand to his mouth. His lips sought her palm, his tongue savouring the salty moisture he found there. Then his eyes focussed on hers and she was suddenly breathless again.

'Isobella.' He said her name huskily, the sound both a protest and a caress. 'This was not meant to happen.'

'I know that.' Isobel shivered. And then, in an attempt to lighten the situation, 'I doubt if you intended to tackle me onto the sofa.'

Alejandro sighed. 'That is not what I meant and you know it,' he told her roughly.

His eyes drifted down over her supine body, lingering sensually on the wedge of pale skin exposed below the hem of her vest. When tumbling her onto the sofa, he must have inadvertently dragged the waistband of her shorts lower, because now he could see the hollow of her navel.

He caught his breath. He knew that if he touched her he wouldn't be responsible for his actions. He was already aroused, and ironically the pain in his leg was eased when he looked at her. Right now, he was fighting the need to spread his hands on her soft skin, to feel her warmth relieving the tension between them.

The curve of her midriff was such a temptation. If he kissed her there, where the indentation of her waist provided a perfect hollow for his lips, would she taste as sweet as he remembered?

He recalled everything about her, that afternoon and

evening in her bed at her apartment, before the phone call from his father had destroyed their relationship: her responsiveness, her passion, her fire. How he'd buried his face against her sex and inhaled the musky fragrance that their love-making had created...

Deus!

He tried to sever his thoughts as completely as his father's phone-call had done, but it was useless. With the proof of her arousal there in the button-hard peaks of her breasts, in the scent of her body rising unmistakeably to his nostrils, she was impossible to resist.

His fists clenched around her forearms as he tried to hold back, but the softness of her skin bruised so easily. Softening his touch, he allowed his fingers to slide from her wrists to the top of her arms. He felt the nerves in her shoulders jump as he caressed her. With every quiver in her muscles, she responded to his touch.

'Tao doce,' he muttered. And then, through his teeth in a final burst of conscience, 'This should not happen.'

'Nothing has happened,' protested Isobel unevenly, but he could tell she didn't believe it.

'It will,' he responded, his voice thickening with emotion. 'Or do you expect me to ignore the evidence your body cannot hide?'

'I— Alejandro...'

But it was too late. He'd already bent his head towards her, capturing one provocative nipple through the thin cotton of her vest.

He sucked on it urgently and Isobel's limbs went weak. Then, between her legs, she felt the unfamiliar gush of wetness. She was on the verge of an orgasm, and he'd hardly touched her!

'Querida,' he said huskily, transferring his attention to her other nipple. 'You are wearing too many clothes.'

Once again, he sucked on her, his tongue seeking a satisfaction only she could give him. Then, with an oath, he forced the offending vest up above her breasts.

'*Melhor,*' he whispered. 'Better. *Muito melhor.* Much better.' He lowered his mouth again, and this time she felt as if his hungry tongue was draining all the strength from her body.

His mouth sought hers now, his teeth capturing the flesh on the inner side of her lower lip. He bit her, not painfully but intimately, before allowing his tongue to make an erotic exploration of its own.

Isobel moaned. She couldn't help it. She was drowning in a sea of sexuality, and when his hands slid beneath her hips to cup her buttocks she arched eagerly towards him.

At first his fingers slid beneath her shorts, tightening the cuffs around her. But then, impatient with the constriction, he pushed the shorts down her legs. He was pleased to discover she was as naked underneath as he'd anticipated, and, after he tugged the vest over her head, she was soon totally exposed.

'*Bela,*' he said hoarsely. 'Beautiful.' He stroked a searching finger from her navel down over the slight swell of her belly and into the moist heart of her womanhood. '*Muita bela.*'

Isobel jerked against his invasion, and in a strangled voice she said, 'Please—please don't.'

'*Nao?*'

'No.' Isobel trembled. 'Not—not yet.'

Alejandro bent to allow his tongue to follow his fingers, and she convulsed violently. 'You do not mean that,' he said confidently, and Isobel's hands sought the buckle of his jeans.

'You—' she said unsteadily. '*You're* wearing too many clothes.'

Alejandro stilled. 'Believe me, you do not mean that,' he said tightly. 'But if you turn off the lights…'

'No.' Isobel levered herself up onto one hand and gripped his wrist with the other. 'Do you think I care what you look like?'

'I care,' he said flatly, but she scrambled out from under him. On her knees in front of him, she began unbuttoning his shirt with studied determination.

'Nao!'

His hands stopped her, but she met his dark gaze without flinching.

'Yes,' she said firmly, freeing her fingers and cupping his face between them. Then, setting her mouth against the dry ridge of his scar, she breathed, 'Trust me, Alejandro. I won't let you down.'

But she would; Alejandro knew it. Knew he'd be a fool to trust any woman. Hadn't she and Miranda proved that? But, with her bare breasts invading that part of his shirt that she'd managed to unfasten, rubbing sensually against the hair on his chest, he found himself stifling his protest, telling himself it was too late to resist her now.

Bearing her back against the cushions of the sofa, he silenced the voices in his head that warned him he was going to regret this. With the hungry pressure of his mouth against hers, he gave himself up to his body's demands.

His shirt came free of his trousers and he felt her pushing it off his shoulders. If she winced at the sight of the scars that were like spiderwebs across his shoulder, he didn't hear her, and when her fingers returned to the buckle of his belt he didn't stop her.

He let her pull the belt free, let her unfasten the button at his waist, her fingers unbearably sensual against his taut flesh. Then his zip slid down and she pushed both his jeans and his silk underwear away and allowed his bulging erection to spill, unfettered, into her hands.

And—*Deus!*—it was good, so good, to feel her holding him. She caressed him, causing him to suck in a breath of protest as she bent and took him into her mouth.

Cristo, he could hardly breathe; hardly dared to breathe, he acknowledged helplessly, aware that he was in danger of totally losing himself.

The driving need he'd been fighting ever since he'd come here was burning like liquid fire in his veins and he knew it. There was no way he either could or would back off now. The feeling of her body next to his, the erotic slide of her tongue, were like exotic signposts to his own personal nirvana. He wanted her; that was a given. And, whatever happened afterwards, he had to have her.

Sliding his fingers into her hair, he forced her head up, feeling the coolness of the air where moments earlier her tongue had been hot against his shaft. He knew he wanted to be inside her, where her heat and her fire would carry all his resistance away.

'Alejandro,' she breathed huskily, arching back on one elbow so that he was given an uninterrupted view of her slender body. Her breasts were rosy-tipped and swollen where he had been sucking them, and the honey-blonde curls between her legs were already moist from the invasion of his tongue.

Without giving another thought to the torn ligaments that disfigured his leg, or the care with which he usually removed his clothes, he thrust his jeans down to his ankles. He shoved off his boots as he did so, allowing him to kick his legs free.

He saw Isobel looking at him, but there was no point in trying to hide his scars. Still, he managed not to grit his teeth too obviously when a pain shot hotly up his thigh.

Besides, Isobel's attention was riveted on his rampant shaft, that rose thick and powerfully male from its nest of dark hair. And he didn't have to be ashamed of that.

'Say it,' he said, capturing her hands in his when she would have touched him again. 'Say you want me. Tell me, Isobella. I want you to have no doubts this time.'

Isobel gazed up into his dark, tormented face, her eyes wide and unknowingly provocative. 'I had no doubts last time,' she murmured, barely audibly, and guessed he didn't hear her. Which was probably just as well. 'I do want you, Alejandro,' she assured him huskily. 'Is that what you needed to hear?'

'Yes,' he said roughly, lowering his head to the cluster of curls between her legs and parting her folds with his tongue again. 'It is what I needed to hear,' he agreed, the faint stubble on his jawline absurdly sensual against her sensitive flesh. 'Ah, *cara*, you are so ready for me.' He glanced up at her, a trace of humour curling his mouth. 'I wonder—shall I make you wait?'

Isobel's breathing felt as if it was suspended, but she managed to say softly, 'Can you?' and he rose over her before covering her mouth with his.

As he did so, the throbbing head of his erection probed her moist core. Isobel spread her legs encouragingly. It was a provocative invitation, and Alejandro was not immune to her appeal. 'You know I cannot,' he said unsteadily. 'Help me, *cara*.' He caught his breath. '*Deus*; that feels so good.'

With her soft hands guiding him, he pressed into her. She was tight, so tight, but her muscles expanded around him, making it seem as if she had been made for just this purpose.

When he had achieved total penetration, he remained still for a moment, enjoying the sensation of her heat surrounding him. He remembered that other occasion when he'd made love to her, and acknowledged with a pang that no matter how many women he'd known, either before or since, he'd never experienced the same satisfaction with anyone else.

'Alejandro,' she whispered now, winding her arms about his neck and pulling his face down to hers. 'Love me, Alejandro.'

He watched her then, watched as he withdrew almost to the point of separation, before thrusting into her again. She moaned in enjoyment, winding one leg around his hip and allowing the sole of her foot to slide sensuously against his calf.

It was an erotic caress, and Alejandro found himself unable to control his movements. Almost without his volition, his body quickened its pace, stroking in and out with an urgency that only enhanced his pleasure as well as her own.

When he felt the first faint stirrings of her orgasm rippling around him, he groaned his approval. Her body spasmed, tightened, dragging him to the brink. Then, with the liquid heat of her essence spilling around him, he could hold back no longer.

With one final thrust, and a sense of fulfilment that was more than mere pleasure, he reached his climax. Drained, satiated, totally content for the first time in a little over three years...

Awareness of his surroundings came slowly.

He didn't usually sleep with lamps still burning, he acknowledged, yet the light in the room wasn't daylight, and his aching body told him that he had had no rest.

Yet, for all that, some of the frustration he often felt upon waking had been eased. And the ache in his thighs wasn't from riding a horse, but a whole different exhaustion entirely.

Isobel. *Isobella*.

He shifted awkwardly, rolling onto his side and gazing somewhat confusedly around the room. Where was she? And how had she got out from under him without waking him? He normally slept so fitfully. He couldn't believe he hadn't known that she'd gone.

But, of course, he hadn't. Wincing slightly, he swung his legs over the side of the sofa and ran frustrated hands through his hair.

Then, looking down at his naked body, he thought he knew why she hadn't waited to share those post-intimacy moments. *Deus*, dismissing his appearance in the heat of the moment was one thing—coping with his scars in cold blood was something else.

Dragging his hands down his face, he got heavily to his feet. Then, rescuing his jeans from the floor, he hauled them on without ceremony. He was desperate to conceal his injuries before he saw Isobel again, and he stuffed his silk boxers into his back pocket, unwilling to risk being caught without his trousers.

His shirt came next, and he was buttoning it up when he heard a sound behind him. Isobel was standing in the bedroom doorway, a towelling bathrobe bulking around her.

He was relieved to see that the blinds at the windows were drawn. At least he didn't have to worry about having an audience, though he had to admit that until now he hadn't even thought of it.

'Hi,' she said, her voice a little shaky. 'Are you okay?'

'Why would I not be?' Alejandro countered, his frustration colouring his tone. His lips twisted. 'What does one say in situations like this—I seem to have overstayed my welcome?'

Isobel's pale face lost all colour. 'You were asleep,' she said defensively. 'I didn't like to disturb you.'

'*Nao?*' Alejandro was sardonic. He glanced blindly at his watch. 'Did I sleep long?'

Isobel's tongue circled her upper lip. 'A little while,' she replied offhandedly, and Alejandro sucked in a breath.

His eyes sought his watch again, and this time he focussed on the dial. It was after two o'clock. He must have slept for a good two hours.

'I am sorry,' he said, aghast. He had obviously been dead to the world. He glanced impatiently about him. 'I must go.'

Isobel didn't say anything. She just stood there, looking at him, and he felt the unwilling pull of her attraction all over again.

However this time he had more sense than to act on it. What they'd shared had been amazing, incredible—but, like that interlude in London, it had been an experience out of time, unlikely to be repeated.

And yet…

He walked haltingly towards the door, steeling himself against the urge to drag his aching leg. He was intensely conscious of her eyes upon him, and he had some pride left.

Then, before opening the door, he turned and said a little stiffly, 'I should have asked you: how is the interview going?'

Isobel's eyes went wide. She couldn't believe he would ask her such a thing, not now, not at this moment. Was he completely insensitive? Well, she thought, she had the answer to that.

Biting back the bitter retort that sprang to her lips, she said tightly, 'Well. It's going well.'

Alejandro's eyes were suddenly intent on hers. 'And

when do you expect to leave?' he asked, aware that he was gripping the handle of the door so hard it was digging into his palm.

'Oh.' Isobel swallowed. 'I—I don't know.'

'But not yet,' he persisted, and she wondered why it mattered to him.

Then she thought of Emma, and once again she was sure she understood.

Understood, too, that for the past few hours she had barely thought of her daughter. And that was unforgiveable.

'Perhaps you ought to ask Senhora Silveira,' she responded, holding the lapels of her robe close about her throat.

Then, because she didn't see why he should have it all his own way, 'Are you going?'

'Oh. *Que? E claro*. What? Of course.' He was startled into speech, automatically using his own language as he struggled to face the fact that she was as eager to end this awkward exchange as he was. 'We will speak again tomorrow, *sim*?'

Isobel held up her head. 'If that's what you want.'

'It is what I want,' he said heavily, and this time he did open the door. '*Boa noite*, Isobella.' He paused. 'Try not to hate me too much, hmm?'

Isobel gasped. 'I don't hate you,' she protested, wondering where that had come from. But Alejandro merely gave her a rather cynical smile before closing the door behind him.

CHAPTER THIRTEEN

IT WAS another two days before Alejandro was able to return to the Villa Mimosa.

The day following his visit to see Isobel, he'd had to fly down to Rio to attend a shareholders' meeting, and then in the evening he'd been roped into a family dinner. In consequence, it was the afternoon of the following day before he was able to fly back to Montevista.

He'd considered driving down to Porto Verde that evening. But, remembering the awkwardness of his departure, he'd decided it would be easier if, when he and Isobel met again, it was daylight.

While the attractions of visiting her rooms again were undeniable, it would probably be wiser and less painful if he maintained a certain detachment until he could gauge how she really felt about him.

He'd thought about her constantly—his attention at the shareholders' meeting had been sadly lacking because of it—and on reflection he was inclined to wonder if he had been too hasty in his assessment of the situation. His gut tightened at the thought. Was it possible that she didn't hate him after all?

Whatever, they could still be civil with one another, he argued—for their daughter's sake, if nothing else.

Because, although he was reluctant to introduce himself to the child until she was older and could understand, he did want to keep in touch with her.

Thank heavens for the Internet, he thought fervently as he drove through the gates of the Villa Mimosa. Without it, he doubted he'd ever have seen Isobel again, or learned that she had had a baby which might conceivably be his child.

He didn't know what he'd expected that boring afternoon in his office at the Cabral building in Rio, when, in an impulsive moment, he'd Googled her name. Certainly not the almost immediate connection to a certain Isobel Jameson who worked for *Lifestyles* magazine.

Even then, he'd hardly been able to believe his luck. But the website for the magazine had published a series of passport-sized photographs of its contributors, and Isobel's face had been instantly recognisable.

Additionally, they'd provided a potted biography. And Alejandro had read incredulously that she had a little girl, named Emma, who he'd subsequently discovered had been born exactly nine months after their brief but oh-so-memorable affair.

At first, he'd been bitterly angry, willing to blame Isobel for the fact that he'd as yet played no part in his daughter's life. The pictures his investigator had emailed him had proved without a doubt that Emma was his child, and he'd badly wanted to confront Isobel and demand his rights.

Time, of course, had made him more prudent. He'd realised the dangers of precipitating their meeting, and that was when the idea of persuading Anita that she should consider giving another interview had been born. However disloyal his intentions had been, he'd consoled himself with the thought that the end justified the means.

Perhaps he should have confided in Anita, he reflected now as the rooftops of Porto Verde appeared below him. But, since Miranda's death, she'd begun to depend on him more and more, and he knew she'd never condone what he planned to do.

Anita had conveniently forgotten so much about her daughter. And her daughter's marriage, brief though it had been, had assumed a tender poignancy in Anita's mind. Which was ridiculous, considering Miranda had never shaken her drug habit and she had only married Alejandro because she'd been consumed with guilt.

Why had he married Miranda, then? Alejandro scowled. If his father hadn't been ill, would he have resisted her pleas? Or had pity—both for her and for himself—played its part? If he had seen himself as some kind of saviour, in the end he'd had to concede defeat.

But that was all in the past, Alejandro reminded himself. He didn't blame Miranda for what had happened: he blamed himself. He should have forced her to get out of the car.

Of course, his own family hadn't seen it that way. Roberto Cabral had never forgiven himself for encouraging his son to get involved with Miranda in the first place. And, though he hadn't actually opposed the marriage, he'd been horrified when afterwards Alejandro had had to tell him that it was unlikely he would ever father a child.

The gates of the Villa Mimosa loomed ahead of him and Alejandro swung into the drive, lifting a hand in acknowledgement to one of the gardeners working in the grounds. Anita didn't allow anyone to shirk their duties, he thought drily, wondering if she and Isobel were managing to control their mutual antipathy to one another.

He would soon find out. Anita was not the kind of person to hide her feelings...

* * *

'So what are you going to do?'

Isobel's aunt regarded her expectantly from across the tack room at Villiers, the estate that Isobel had always regarded as her home. Olivia and Emma were supposed to be oiling the saddles, but the little girl was getting as much oil on her hands as she was on anything else.

Isobel bent to wipe her daughter's fingers and then looked up at the other woman with a rueful sigh. 'I don't know, do I? That's why I'm asking you. Do you think I should try and get in touch with him again?'

Olivia shook her head. 'What do you want to do? Do you want to see him again?'

'Of course I do.' Isobel was impatient. 'But, well, it's complicated.'

Olivia shrugged. 'Did you sleep with him?'

'Aunt Olivia!'

'Well, bite me, but that's the only complication I can think of.'

'Well, it's not.' But Isobel's cheeks had deepened with colour. 'I just think he only engineered the interview because of Emma.'

'The interview you allowed the Silveira woman to walk away from,' remarked Olivia drily. 'You were a fool, Isobel. You should have insisted on seeing Alejandro before you left.'

'And how was I supposed to do that?' Isobel was indignant. 'I had no way of getting to Montevista, and I didn't know his phone number. Besides, Anita wanted me to leave immediately.'

'I bet she did!'

'And I could hardly stay at the airport until Alejandro chose to appear. If he did appear at all.'

Olivia shrugged, rescuing the bottle of oil from Emma's grimy fingers and taking the little girl's hand in hers.

'Come on,' she said, speaking to the child. 'Let's get those hands clean. And then we'll go and see about some lunch.'

'Aunt Olivia…'

'Mummy wash Emma's hands,' protested the little girl, squirming away from the older woman. Clutching her mother's coat, she added, 'You do it, Mummy. Not 'Livia.'

Isobel grimaced at the dirty marks now decorating her midi-length duster-coat. It was her own fault for wearing such a light colour to visit the stables. 'Okay, Tuppence,' she said, grasping her daughter's fingers before they did any more damage. 'Let's all go back to the house.'

The three of them trudged back to the house through the remains of the snow that had fallen the previous evening. Although it was already the middle of February, there was no sign of winter relaxing its grip. Only the daffodils flowering in the borders promised a taste of springtime, white-headed snowdrops pushing through the snow.

Isobel wrapped the folds of her coat about her. Since returning from Brazil, she'd felt the cold more severely, and was only just recovering from a nasty cough. In her all-in-one woolly jumpsuit, Emma was snug and cosy, while Olivia was wearing her usual jeans with a sweater and a warm Barbour jacket.

It wasn't until they rounded the potting shed and entered the shrubbery that Isobel saw the black Audi parked on the drive. A huge four-by-four, it dominated her small Mazda, which she'd used to drive down from London the previous day.

'Now, who can that be?' her aunt asked half-impatiently. 'If Sam was expecting guests for lunch, he should have told me. As it is, I doubt I've got anything suitable to offer them.'

'You've always got something suitable,' retorted Isobel wryly. 'Mrs Collins always says you buy too much food.'

'Mrs Collins is a daily woman, not a housekeeper,'

replied Olivia, unzipping her jacket as they entered the bootroom that adjoined the kitchen. Generally, she prepared all the family's meals herself. Then she clicked her tongue, 'Oh, I know who it will be—Tony Aitken. I'd heard he was back from his skiing trip, and I told Nora you'd be pleased to see him.'

'You're not serious!' Isobel groaned as she helped Emma off with her jumpsuit. 'Heavens, Aunt Olivia, why would you say a thing like that?'

'Because since you got back from Brazil you've done nothing but mope around the house,' declared Olivia briskly, and Isobel gave her an indignant look.

'I've not been well since I got home!' she exclaimed. 'I've had a cold and a cough; you know that.'

'Since when has a cold and a cough laid you low?' demanded her aunt blandly. 'I don't know what happened, Isobel. You seem very loath to discuss it. But it seems to me that if you and Alejandro are not going to see one another again—'

'I didn't say that.'

'As good as,' continued her aunt, undeterred. 'Anyway, I think it would do you good to spend time with another man. One whose life isn't *complicated*, as you put it.'

Isobel sighed. 'You don't understand.'

'So you did sleep with him.' Olivia made a smug face. Then she frowned suspiciously. 'I hope you took precautions this time.'

Fortunately, Emma chose that moment to trip over her boots and sprawl on the floor of the bootroom. She burst into tears, of course, and Isobel was able to hide her flushed face against the little girl's hair.

'It's okay,' she said, cuddling her close, loving the distinctive smell of prolonged babyhood. 'Come on. Let's go and see if Mrs Collins has a chocolate in her drawer.'

Whatever else Olivia might have said was happily aborted. Picking Emma up, Isobel opened the kitchen door and stepped into the warmth of the room. An Aga heated the large cooking-area, and concealed lights below the wall-cupboards gave the room a snug and cosy appearance.

Mrs Collins turned from where she'd obviously been making a pot of coffee. 'Mr Armstrong has a guest,' she said in explanation. 'I asked him if he'd like me to make some coffee, and he said yes.'

'Oh, thank you, Hilda.' Olivia came to look enquiringly over her shoulder. 'Mmm; that smells good. Would you like me to take it in?'

'If you would, Mrs Armstrong.' Mrs Collins stepped back from the tray she'd been preparing with some relief. 'My arthritis has been playing up and I wouldn't like to trust my shoulder. Are you sure you can manage? Perhaps Isobel can give you a hand.'

'After we've got these little paws clean,' said Isobel, displaying Emma's fingers for the woman to see. Anything to delay joining Tony and her uncle. Could she possibly invent a headache and leave them to it?

'Give her here!' exclaimed Mrs Collins, holding out her arms invitingly. 'I've got some special soap we can use, Emma, and then maybe there'll be a chocolate for a good girl. What do you say?'

Emma nodded, wriggling out of her mother's arms and allowing Mrs Collins to carry her into the cloakroom next door. 'Bye, Mummy,' she called, her tears forgotten, and Isobel had no choice but to accompany her aunt out into the hall.

'Cheer up,' said Olivia, noticing Isobel's tight expression. 'For heaven's sake, you can be polite, can't you? I'm not asking you to marry him!'

'Just as well,' muttered Isobel, barely audibly, as her aunt opened the door into the sitting room. She needed time to think over what she was going to do about Alejandro, not waste time making small talk with Tony Aitken.

The two men were seated at either side of the hearth, where a log fire burned brightly. Although the house was centrally heated, both her aunt and uncle liked an open fire, and Isobel moved towards it automatically, paying little attention to the occupants of the two armchairs.

Olivia carried in the tray and set it down on the low table between them. Both men rose to their feet as she did so and then, almost subconsciously, Isobel heard her aunt suck in her breath.

'Oh my goodness,' she said with evident embarrassment. 'You startled me.'

Isobel was already turning when she heard his response.

'Regrettably, I do that to people,' he said apologetically, but already her aunt was making amends.

'No, I mean—you're so big!' she exclaimed with a girlish little giggle that Isobel had never heard before. 'I was expecting to see Tony—Tony Aitken. A friend of Isobel's. And he certainly isn't as tall as you.'

Alejandro's lips tightened at the mention of the other man's name, but he managed to stretch them into a smile. 'You must be Isobella's Aunt Olivia,' he said after a beat. 'How do you do, *senhora*? It is a pleasure to meet you.'

'And to meet you—um, Alejandro, isn't it?' Olivia was enthusiastic, and Isobel stood there feeling as if all her bones had suddenly turned to water. Olivia's smile was warm. 'I don't think anyone else calls my niece Isobella.'

Alejandro pulled a wry face. 'It is a—what do you say?—a weakness of mine, *senhora*. My grandmother's name was Isobella also.'

'Really?'

Isobel could see that her aunt was totally fascinated by him. Far from flinching at the sight of his scar, she was positively blossoming under his undivided attention.

For her part, Isobel was staring at him as if she couldn't quite believe her eyes. In black jeans and dark-grey cashmere jacket, over a black silk shirt that was open at the neck, he was so heartachingly familiar. Oh, *why* had he come here? Not just to see his daughter, she prayed.

It was only when her uncle spoke that she dragged her gaze away to survey her own less-than-polished appearance. She was still wearing the coat with Emma's fingermarks all over the skirt. And, although the coat was open, her green-and-blue-striped tee-shirt and shabby denim mini were hardly high fashion.

Her eyes darted to Alejandro again, as her uncle was bidding their guest to resume his seat. And this time he caught her gaze, his amber eyes narrowed and intent. Her breathing stilled, her throat drying as he continued to look at her. What was he thinking? she wondered. What had he been saying to her uncle before she and Olivia had interrupted them?

And then the door crashed open again and a small girl erupted into the room. In a woolly sweater and cotton dungarees, she was absolutely adorable. Alejandro, whose gaze had been distracted from Isobel at her entrance, now stared at the child in helpless fascination.

Emma, he thought. His daughter. *Their* daughter—his and Isobel's. *Meu Deus, but she is beautiful.* As dark-haired as he was, but with Isobel's peachy-soft complexion.

Not that Isobel had any colour in her face at this moment. He'd heard her catch her breath at the child's entrance and understood her concern. In all honesty, it wasn't the way he would have chosen to meet his daughter. But it was too late now to be having second thoughts.

Now, however, Emma's attention was focussed on him, and she came towards him without any apparent reluctance on her part. 'Who're you?' she asked, her eyes wide and inquisitive, and Alejandro felt his stomach twist with sudden apprehension.

'My name is Alejandro,' he said. He had risen to his feet again at her entrance, but now he lowered himself to the child's level with an effort. 'Who are you?'

'I'm Emma,' she said. Then she pointed to his face. 'What's that? Did you fall over?'

Alejandro's lips twitched. 'Something like that,' he agreed ruefully.

'Does it hurt?'

'Emma!'

Both Isobel and her aunt spoke in unison, but Alejandro made a gesture warning the two women not to interfere.

'No, *cara*,' he said gently, speaking to the child. 'It does not hurt.' He paused. 'It happened a long time ago.'

Emma frowned, still staring at him, and then she reached out a hand towards his cheek.

'Emma!'

This time Isobel had to intervene, but before she could grab the little girl's arm Alejandro had bent his head obligingly towards her.

''S hard!' Emma exclaimed in surprise, her baby-soft fingers stroking along the ridge of his scar. 'Feel, Mummy. 'S re'lly hard.'

Alejandro looked up at Isobel's pale face before getting heavily to his feet.

'Forgive me,' he said, his attention all on her now. 'I did not come here to upset you.'

Isobel swallowed with difficulty. And then, because

she couldn't think of anything else to say at that moment, she whispered, 'I told you Emma wasn't easily alarmed.'

'And you were right,' Alejandro murmured softly. 'Perhaps one day you might even tell her who I am.'

CHAPTER FOURTEEN

'YOU'RE not leaving!'

There was a trace of panic in Isobel's voice now, and although Emma was tugging at her skirt, wanting her attention, for the first time in her life Isobel didn't put her daughter's needs first.

Alejandro looked down at the little girl. 'Perhaps not yet,' he conceded gently, allowing Emma to grab his hand.

'Up,' she said imperiously, her meaning obvious, and with a feeling of incredulity he lifted the little girl into his arms.

'Mummy's talking, Em,' admonished Isobel, feeling as if the situation was slipping away from her.

'I talk too,' retorted Emma, regarding Alejandro's face with renewed interest. Her brows drew together consideringly. 'D'you fall off your pony?'

'I don't think Mr Cabral wants to talk about that now, Emma,' declared Sam Armstrong, giving their guest a rueful look. He held out his arms. 'Come along, sweetheart. I think we need to give Mummy a chance to talk.'

Emma clung to Alejandro's jacket. 'Don' wanna go,' she pouted, but Olivia stepped forward and took control.

'It's lunchtime,' she said firmly, loosening the little girl's fingers with a word of apology to Alejandro. Then, lifting her out of his arms, she continued, 'Do join us for lunch, Alejandro. I can't promise you anything special, but you're very welcome to stay.'

'Thank you.'

Alejandro inclined his head, though whether that was just politeness or acceptance Isobel couldn't be sure. But she was grateful when the door closed behind them. Even if being alone with him was still a daunting prospect.

'Um, why don't you sit down again?' she suggested, gesturing to the chair behind him. She was sure his leg must be aching by now.

'I am not an invalid, *cara*,' he said flatly, making no move to do as she'd asked. He paused, regarding her intently. 'Are you well?'

'I've had a cold, that's all.' Isobel didn't want to talk about herself. Then, because her legs were decidedly unsteady, she sank into the armchair her uncle had been occupying and looked up at him. 'When did you get here?'

'Here?' Alejandro pointed to where she was standing. 'Or do you mean England?'

Isobel shrugged. 'Both, I guess.' She was disturbed to find there were tears pricking at the backs of her eyes and she blinked rapidly. 'You should have let me know you were coming.'

'Why?' Alejandro shifted his weight onto his uninjured leg. 'So you could have arranged not to be here?'

'No!' Isobel caught her breath. 'I wanted to see you.' She hesitated. 'If only to—to tell you why I came back to England.'

'Ah.' Alejandro's expression was sardonic. 'I think Anita told me that.'

'Did she? I doubt it.' Isobel sounded bitter. 'She terminated the interview, you know. Not me.'

'Did she tell you why?'

Isobel frowned. 'Well, she said she'd never have agreed to it if it hadn't been for you.' She averted her eyes. 'But I already knew that, didn't I?'

'And that was all?'

'No.' Isobel took a deep breath. 'She told me she didn't like the idea of having a "snake in the grass" in her house. Those were her words, not mine. Apparently the fact that you and I had known one another in London didn't sit well with her. She accused me of only accepting the assignment to see you again.'

'Mmm.' Alejandro was thoughtful. 'So she did not mention the fact that she knew I had visited your rooms the night before? That one of her minions had been positioned outside the window while we were otherwise engaged?'

'No!' Isobel was horrified. 'You mean she—?'

'Knew we had been together? Well, maybe not all the details, but she knew enough.'

'My God!'

'*Sim— Meu Deus!*'

Isobel shook her head. 'But why should it matter to her? Unless she—'

'Do not go there,' Alejandro advised heavily, giving in to his leg's weakness and sinking down onto the edge of the chair opposite. 'Anita has never been anything more to me than my mother-in-law. If she is jealous, it is because she wants to guard her daughter's reputation. She cannot bear the thought that I might find happiness with someone else.'

Isobel's coat fell to the floor at either side of her and she smoothed suddenly damp palms over her knees. 'With me?' she whispered, and it was barely audible.

'Who else?' he responded quietly. 'Until we met again, she knew I had had no intention of getting involved with anyone else.'

Isobel shook her head. 'Does she know about Emma?'

'She does now.'

'You told her?'

'Of course.' He was dismissive. 'She had already put it all together herself.'

Isobel blew out a breath. 'No wonder she wanted me to leave.'

Alejandro pulled a wry face. 'No wonder,' he echoed. 'Of course, if you had wanted to stay, you could have made other arrangements.'

Isobel gasped. 'What other arrangements?'

'You could have told me,' he said heavily. 'Or did I figure so low on your list of possibilities that it did not even occur to you to do so?'

Isobel sprang to her feet. 'That's ridiculous, and you know it.'

'Do I?'

'You should,' she said, the treacherous prick of tears burning her eyes again. 'How was I supposed to speak to you? Should I have asked Anita for your phone number? I'm sure she would have given it to me—not!'

Alejandro looked up at her, his tawny eyes dark and assessing. 'It did not occur to you to hire a car and driver and come to the *estancia*?'

'I couldn't do that!' Isobel stared at him in amazement. 'What would I have done if I'd turned up at your door and you'd turned me away too?'

Alejandro's jaw hardened, and, placing his hands on the arms of the chair, he pushed himself determinedly to his feet. 'I would not have turned you away,' he said harshly. 'How can you suggest such a thing? You are the mother of my daughter; the mother of the only child I am ever likely to have.'

Isobel blinked. 'What do you mean?'

'What do you think I mean?' Alejandro shifted impatiently. 'The accident did not only disfigure me externally, but internally too.'

'Oh, Alejandro!' Isobel thought she was beginning to understand. 'So that was why you were so keen to rekindle our relationship?'

'What do you mean?' he demanded now, as she had only moments before.

'I mean, it's not me you really care about, is it?' she choked, her tears uncontrollable now. 'You want Emma; you want your daughter. And you're prepared to go to any lengths to get her.'

Alejandro stepped back, raking long fingers through his hair as he stared at her in disbelief. 'You really believe that?' he demanded, aghast.

Isobel didn't know what she believed. She'd thrown the accusation at him in the heat of the moment, but in her heart of hearts she prayed it wasn't true.

'Well it—it fits the facts, doesn't it?' she stammered, wiping the heels of her hands across her wet cheeks. 'You—you knew all about Emma before I came to Brazil. You accused me of keeping her existence from you.'

'Which you did,' pointed out Alejandro levelly. 'But, on reflection, I do not think I can entirely blame you for that.'

'Oh, thanks!'

She sniffed, and Alejandro said harshly, 'Do not be facetious. There is much more than our daughter's existence between us and you know it.'

'Do I?' Isobel scrubbed the back of her hand under her nose, wishing she had more control.

'You should,' said Alejandro roughly. 'Would you like me to prove it? Yet I do not think your aunt and uncle would approve if I threw you down onto their hearth-rug and made mad, passionate love to you, do you?'

'You're making fun of me.'

'No, I am not.'

Isobel shook her head, turning away, unable to sustain this unequal contest of wills. 'Oh, I know you can make me do what you want,' she mumbled unsteadily. 'I know you know you've only got to kiss me and I'm like putty in your hands.'

'Do I know that?' Alejandro's voice had changed, deepened, and suddenly his hands were warm upon her shoulders. He drew her back against his muscled frame. 'You have never told me, *cara*. Exactly what do I mean to you?'

Isobel moved her head helplessly from side to side. 'You know,' she insisted. 'You've always known.'

'No,' he said hoarsely, close to her ear. 'No, I have not. Tell me, *cara*. Why are you crying—because you care about me, or because you are afraid I might try to take Emma from you?'

Isobel glanced quickly over her shoulder. 'Would you do that?' she asked anxiously, and Alejandro wearily shook his head.

'If you have to ask me that, then you do not know me at all,' he told her flatly, releasing her. He stepped back. 'Relax, *cara*. Emma is safe. I would not to do anything that might jeopardise her—or your—future.'

He turned, bending to lift a dark overcoat that she now saw was draped over the back of his chair. 'Please—tell your aunt I cannot accept her so kind inv—'

'Don't go!'

Isobel moved now, catching his arm before he could push it into the sleeve of his overcoat, snatching the overcoat from him and tossing it back onto the chair.

'Please,' she said when he remained still, just staring at her. 'I'm sorry. I know you would never hurt me.' She caught her lower lip between her teeth. 'I don't know why

I asked you that.' She sniffed again. 'Just—just jealous, I guess.'

'Jealous?' His dark brows descended.

'Yes.' She pressed her lips together for a moment and then went on, 'Of Emma. Because you love her. Because you care about her in a way that you've never cared about me.'

Alejandro swore then. 'How do you know that?'

'Well, it's obvious, isn't it? I mean—' She chose her words with care. 'Even after you got out of hospital you didn't come back to England.' She paused, and then added painfully, 'You married Miranda, remember?'

'As if I could forget,' murmured Alejandro with feeling. '*Meu Deus*, Isobella, do you really think I did not want to see you again?'

'Then why?'

'Need you ask?' Alejandro scowled. 'When I got out of hospital I thought no woman in her right mind would want to spend the rest of her life with me.'

'But that's crazy!'

'Is it? Well, maybe it seems so now, but at the time I was not thinking so clearly.' He sighed. 'Besides, although we had been intimate, we hardly knew one another. How could I expect you to take on this burden? Particularly when we had parted on such unfriendly terms.'

'You mean the phone call from your father?'

'Yes. That phone call.' Alejandro drew a deep breath. 'I know I told you it was about the company, but it was actually about Miranda. My late wife was an addict, Isobella. She spent her life going in and out of clinics trying to kick her habit. But she never did.'

Isobel was silent for a moment. Then she said softly, 'I didn't know that.'

'No. How could you? Anita did everything she could

to keep it quiet. Even my own family would not accept that a cure was hopeless.'

'And Anita was involved, even then?'

'Oh yes.' Alejandro nodded. 'Our families had been friends since Miranda and I were children.' His lips twisted. 'It was Anita who persuaded my father to phone me that evening and beg me to come home. She was of the opinion that I might be able to help Miranda see sense when everyone else had failed.'

'And did you?'

'No.' Alejandro's tone was flat. He paused. 'And then, after the accident...' He lifted his shoulders in a weary gesture. 'I had other things to worry about.'

'But why did you marry her?'

'Ah...' Alejandro grimaced. 'A question I have asked myself more times than I can remember. Because my father had had another heart attack after my accident; because it was expected. Because my father wanted grand-children and I hadn't given him any.'

'But didn't you just say...?'

'That I could not father any more children? That is correct.' He gave a harsh laugh. 'Something I refrained from broadcasting until after the wedding.'

Isobel frowned. 'Did you love Miranda?'

'I was fond of her,' Alejandro conceded honestly. 'As I say, we had known one another since our schooldays.' He paused. 'She desperately wanted to make her mother proud of her, and it certainly stopped people from pitying me because of my scars.'

'Oh, Alejandro...'

Alejandro's senses swam at the sensuous sound of his name on her tongue. His hand sought her chin, tilted her face up to his, and he rubbed the pad of his thumb over her bottom lip with undisguised impatience.

But there were still things to be said between them.

'Even so, I wonder how you would have felt if I had turned up on your doorstep looking like the gargoyle I resembled when I came out of the hospital?' he ventured huskily. 'Whatever you say now, you might have turned me away.'

'No!'

'No?' Alejandro regarded her intently. 'Ah, yes, you were carrying my baby. That might have made a difference.'

'Alejandro, my being pregnant wouldn't have made a scrap of difference.' Isobel sighed frustratedly. 'It's not just the way you look that I, well, that I care about. It's you!'

'So, you really thought we had something special?'

'Don't you?' A tremor ran through her, and he was suddenly struck by the fact that she'd lost weight in these weeks that they'd been apart. 'I thought so then and I thought so that night at the villa,' she continued urgently. 'But you didn't say anything, and when Anita asked me to leave…'

'Indeed.' Alejandro's thumb invaded her lips, and her tongue met it eagerly. 'We have wasted so much time, *cara*.' His eyes darkened. 'And now I hear there is another man in your life.'

'No.' Isobel misunderstood. 'David died!' she exclaimed, but Alejandro only shook his head.

'Not the man who was your husband,' he said tersely. 'He was a fool. And, although I am sorry to hear he died, he is of no interest to me.' His free hand cupped her neck. 'What was the name of the man your aunt spoke of—Tony, *sim*? Should I be jealous?'

'I think you know the answer to that,' said Isobel a little breathlessly. When he was touching her, it was hard to think of anything else. 'But you've taken so long to make up your mind to come here,' she added, lifting a trembling hand and stroking dark, silky hair from his forehead. 'Are you sure there isn't anything you should tell me?'

Alejandro laughed. Then, capturing her hand, he brought it passionately to his mouth. 'Believe me, *querida*,' he said, 'if I had really believed you wanted to see me again, a string of Carlos's horses would not have kept me away.'

His mouth gently brushed hers, but when she would have prolonged the kiss he laid a finger across her lips. 'Have some pity,' he said a little thickly. 'You know I want you. Very badly, *acontece que*. As it happens. But this is not my home. It is yours.'

'And Emma's,' she reminded him softly, and Alejandro pulled her urgently into his arms.

'Our daughter,' he said with feeling. 'Do you think she will forgive me? I mean, of course, for intruding into her life?'

'Oh, I think she can cope,' murmured Isobel lightly. 'I'm so glad you changed your mind about meeting her.'

'I had no choice,' he said simply. 'I realised I could not live without her mother.' He cradled her face in his hands. 'I love you, *querida*. Perhaps that will redeem me in her eyes.'

EPILOGUE

Six months later, Isobel walked out onto the balcony at the *estancia*, feeling the sun warm upon her hot skin.

The view from the balcony always enchanted her—distant mountains and sunlit highlands, plains and a river valley, and so much space.

Tipping her head back, she ran a hand from her bare throat down over the tender peaks of her breasts to the slight mound beneath her ribcage. Despite feeling a little nauseous in the mornings, she had never been healthier. Happiness did that to a person, she thought smugly. And she was happier now than she had ever been in her life.

There was a sound behind her, and she glanced over her shoulder to find Alejandro emerging through the French doors.

He grinned when he saw her, his eyes filled with satisfaction at the knowledge that she was his wife now and no one could ever part them again.

'I missed you,' he said, coming to nuzzle her shoulder. He drew her back against his hard body. 'It is far too early to get up. Why do you not come back to bed?'

Isobel lifted her shoulder to accommodate his lips and then said softly, 'Don't you think you should put some clothes on?'

'It would be a waste of time,' he retorted huskily. 'I would only have to take them off again, *querida*.'

Isobel gave a soft laugh. 'It's just as well I don't follow your example,' she murmured, despite the fact that Alejandro was tipping her satin wrap off her shoulder so that he could nibble her scented flesh.

'Ah, *sim*.' His voice was muffled. 'But you are a beautiful woman, *cara*. I would not want to make my male employees jealous.'

Isobel sucked in a breath of pleasure. 'You're shameless,' she whispered unsteadily, and now Alejandro allowed himself a delighted laugh.

'Shameless?' he echoed. 'Yes, when I am with you, I do not care who sees me. You have done that to me, *cara*. You and Emma both.'

Isobel sighed contentedly. 'I hope she's all right,' she said thoughtfully. Emma was staying with Alejandro's parents in Rio, quite content to be the centre of attention with her new grandparents.

'Well, she and Caterina seem to get along well enough,' replied Alejandro. He pulled a wry face. 'I think the idea that they are so much alike intrigues them both.'

Isobel nodded. 'Remember how angry I was when you showed me that picture of Caterina?'

Alejandro chuckled. 'How could I forget?'

'I suppose it must have been quite a shock, discovering you had a daughter,' Isobel ventured. She slipped her arms around his neck, rising up on her toes so she could press herself against him. 'Have you forgiven me for keeping her existence from you?'

Alejandro grimaced. 'Ah, *cara*,' he said a little roughly. 'I would forgive you anything. Have you not realised that by now?' He bent and captured the lobe of her ear between his lips, his teeth causing a pain that was both sharp and sensual. 'Sometimes I find it so hard to believe I have been given a second chance with you.'

'Oh, *querido*!'

Isobel used the endearment deliberately, knowing he liked it when she used his language. And she was learning. While she still wasn't very good at conversation, she was able to understand a lot of what was said.

Alejandro kissed her then, his mouth hot and hungry, and her head swam with the mindless pleasure he aroused within her. For a moment, she was so consumed by her own body's needs that she forgot what she had been thinking about when he'd joined her. But then, when she felt his erection throbbing urgently against her stomach, she managed to recover her senses.

'Someone might see,' she said breathlessly, but Alejandro only dismissed her fears.

'Let them,' he said, slipping his hands inside her wrap and pulling her naked body against his. '*Deus*; I did not think it was possible to love someone as much as I love you, *mi amor*.'

Isobel smiled, sliding her hands into the lustrous thickness of his dark hair. 'That's nice,' she said teasingly. 'Because, you know, I love you too.' She frowned. 'Maybe just a little bit, anyway.'

Alejandro growled a protest. 'Just a little bit?' he protested, and she rose onto her toes again to bestow a soft kiss at the corner of his mouth.

'Quite a lot, actually,' she admitted. 'But I don't want you to get conceited.'

'Like that would happen.' Alejandro's tone was dry.

'Oh, I don't know.' Isobel was thoughtful. 'I've seen the way Carlos's wife looks at you. I'm sure she secretly thinks you're hot!'

Alejandro pulled a wry face. 'I am equally sure she

does not. But, in any case, we do not have any secrets from one another, *cara*.'

'Don't we?' Isobel arched her brows and he gave her a puzzled look.

'No.'

'Mmm.' Isobel considered his answer. 'You didn't tell me Miranda was driving the car when you had the accident.'

Alejandro groaned. 'Carlos did, I suppose? Does it matter?'

'It matters to me.' Isobel sniffed a little emotionally. 'I think you're far too honourable for your own good.'

'Oh, please.' Alejandro pulled a face. 'I am no hero. When Miranda got into the driving seat of my car that night, what I should have done was haul her out.'

'So why didn't you?'

'Ah…' He expelled a heavy sigh. Then he cupped her cheek with one hand, his finger finding the pulse beating below her ear. 'She told me she wanted to prove that she was clean—you know, free of drugs. And I was foolish enough to let her.'

'What happened?'

He shook his head now. 'Well, she was not clean, of course. I realised that almost immediately. But, when I told her to stop the car, she ignored me.'

'Oh, Alejandro…'

'The accident happened so quickly,' he said, his eyes darkening at the memory. 'She was driving too fast, and I knew we were not going to make the corner. She lost control and the vehicle plunged into a ravine.'

'My God!' Isobel pressed her face against his chest, inhaling his scent with trembling awareness. 'You could have been killed!'

'Yes.' Alejandro pulled another face. 'There were times

in the next few months when I wished I had been,' he admitted. 'Lying in the hospital, I honestly believed my life was over.'

'I'm so glad you survived,' said Isobel fervently, and he felt the hotness of her tears against his skin.

He lifted her face and wiped them away with his thumb. 'That is why being with you is such a miracle,' he told her softly. 'You have totally changed my life.'

'And you mine,' she whispered. And when he kissed her again she gave herself up to the wanton delight of just being in his arms.

With a muffled exclamation, Alejandro caught her hand in his and tugged her back into the bedroom. Then, tumbling her onto the huge bed, he covered her body with his own.

It was a tangible act of possession that had Isobel arching beneath him, winding her legs about his hips until the open invitation she was offering brooked no denial on his part.

With a groan of pleasure, he filled her with his strength and his fire, creating an answering need inside her. It was always like this when they were together, she thought eagerly—an unleashed passion that neither of them could resist.

Afterwards when Alejandro was lying sleepily beside her, one arm lying with proprietary ownership across her midriff, successfully imprisoning her to his side, Isobel murmured softly, 'Tell me what the doctors said about you not being able to father any more children.'

Alejandro groaned. 'Must I?' His eyes opened to regard her appealingly. 'Ask me that some other time.'

'No, I want to know now.' She was infuriatingly insistent. 'It doesn't seem to have interfered with your sexual drive at all.'

'*Agradeça Deus!*' said Alejandro fervently. 'Thank God!' He propped himself up on one elbow to look down at her. 'Surely you knew that?'

'Don't I just?' she said mischievously, stroking a teasing finger down his chest. 'No, I wasn't worried. I had another reason for asking.'

'What?'

'Tell me what the doctors said and I'll tell you.'

'Ah, *Deus!*' Alejandro flopped down onto his back, staring resignedly up at the ceiling. 'I had some internal injuries, as I told you. The doctors were of the opinion that they might have damaged my ability to produce viable sperm.'

Faint colour had invaded his cheeks as he spoke, but now he turned to look at her with defensive eyes. 'Does it matter? I have you. I have Emma. That is enough.'

'Is it?'

'It has to be,' he said harshly. 'Unless you are suggesting something else.'

Isobel's tongue circled her lips. 'Like what?' she asked, and Alejandro swore softly under his breath.

'There are alternatives,' he said flatly. 'If you want other children.'

Isobel smiled then. 'Oh, I want other children,' she said, and he felt as if a knife had been plunged into his stomach. Then she went on amazingly, 'Your children, *querido*.' She watched the confusion fill his face and took pity on him. 'And, if all goes well, we'll have our second child in about five months from now.'

She saw his expression alter. First he looked disbelieving, then stunned, and finally an incredulous look of wonder spread over his face.

'You mean...?'

He couldn't get the words out, and Isobel finished the

sentence for him. 'I mean we're going to have a baby,' she said proudly. 'It seems as if doctors are sometimes wrong.'

Their son was born at the house Alejandro had bought for his family in the Santa Teresa district of Rio some five months later. A sprawling mansion of over thirty rooms, it had an unrivalled view of the *Baia de Guanabara*, or Guanabara Bay, and Isobel loved it.

It was their home, the place where other babies might be conceived. And, although Alejandro still maintained control of the Cabral company, he had delegated a lot of his work to his brother so he could spend as much time as possible with his wife and family.

Emma had taken to life in Brazil with great enthusiasm. Although she didn't call Alejandro 'Daddy' yet, she understood that he played a huge part in her life. The two of them had become close friends since Isobel's pregnancy, and the little girl was forever asking when her baby brother or sister would be born.

Isobel had deliberately asked the doctor not to tell her the sex of the baby. She wanted it to be a complete surprise for the whole family. One of her closest friends now was Marianna, Jose's wife and her sister-in-law. Soon after Isobel's pregnancy had been announced, Marianna had admitted she was pregnant too.

Alejandro himself was present at the birth of his son, and it was he who put the baby into her arms for the first time. 'See?' he said huskily. 'He is so handsome.'

'Just like his father,' said Isobel with feeling, and they shared a smile of total understanding.

'And you,' he said, stroking the damp hair back from her forehead. 'How do you feel? That is the most important thing to me.'

Isobel smiled again. 'Oh, Alejandro, I feel great—and

it was so easy! I told you, you didn't have to worry. I'm obviously stronger than I look.'

Alejandro regarded her adoringly. He felt so grateful to have this beautiful English girl in his life. He couldn't imagine living his life without her now. She had made him whole, and it didn't get any better than that.

'You'll have to phone your mother and Aunt Olivia,' Isobel said after a moment. Alejandro's parents were looking after Emma at the moment, and Uncle Sam and Aunt Olivia were going to come and stay for a few weeks after the birth to give Isobel time to relax.

'I think your wife should get some rest, *senhor*,' said Doctor Fernandez now, moving forward. He and two nurses had been in charge of the delivery, and he gave Alejandro an apologetic look. 'You can come back later, *senhor*. When Senhora Cabral has had some sleep, *nao*?'

Alejandro hesitated, but Isobel caught his hand and squeezed it encouragingly. 'Perhaps that would be best, *querido*,' she said as one of the nurses took the baby from her arms. 'You should ring Anita too. I wouldn't like her to find out from someone else.'

'You are too considerate,' said Alejandro drily. 'But I suppose I do have her to thank for bringing us together.'

'I doubt she'd see it that way,' murmured Isobel, smiling up at him. 'But she has been very kind to me recently.'

'That is because she has realised how nice it is to have a child about the house,' declared Alejandro, ignoring the doctor's evident frustration.

And it was true. Since Anita had met Emma, she had changed enormously. But the little girl would win anyone's heart, thought Alejandro proudly. He glanced round at the nurse laying his son in a bassinette. And soon the little one would be breaking every woman's heart.

'You'd better go,' said Isobel, aware of Doctor Fernandez hovering behind him. 'But come back soon, won't you? I'm going to get up later on.'

'If you're sure.'

But Alejandro was in no hurry to leave her. Bending his head, he bestowed a warm, lingering kiss on her mouth. His family, he thought, with renewed amazement. He was so lucky. In fact, he decided, he was the luckiest man in the world...

* * * * *

*Harlequin Intrigue top author Delores Fossen presents
a brand-new series of breathtaking romantic suspense!*
TEXAS MATERNITY: HOSTAGES
*The first installment available May 2010:
THE BABY'S GUARDIAN*

Shaw cursed and hooked his arm around Sabrina.

Despite the urgency that the deadly gunfire created, he tried to be careful with her, and he took the brunt of the fall when he pulled her to the ground. His shoulder hit hard, but he held on tight to his gun so that it wouldn't be jarred from his hand.

Shaw didn't stop there. He crawled over Sabrina, sheltering her pregnant belly with his body, and he came up ready to return fire.

This was obviously a situation he'd wanted to avoid at all cost. He didn't want his baby in the middle of a fight with these armed fugitives, but when they fired that shot, they'd left him no choice. Now, the trick was to get Sabrina safely out of there.

"Get down," someone on the SWAT team yelled from the roof of the adjacent building.

Shaw did. He dropped lower, covering Sabrina as best he could.

There was another shot, but this one came from a rifleman on the SWAT team. Shaw didn't look up, but he heard the sound of glass being blown apart.

The shots continued, all coming from his men, which meant it might be time to try to get Sabrina to better cover. Shaw glanced at the front of the building.

So that Sabrina's pregnant belly wouldn't be smashed against the ground, Shaw eased off her and moved her to a sitting position so that her back was against the brick wall. They were close. Too close. And face-to-face.

He found himself staring right into those sea-green eyes.

How will Shaw get Sabrina out?
Follow the daring rescue and the heartbreaking
aftermath in THE BABY'S GUARDIAN
by Delores Fossen,
available May 2010 from Harlequin Intrigue.

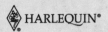
® HARLEQUIN®

INTRIGUE®

REQUEST YOUR FREE BOOKS!

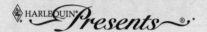 HARLEQUIN® *Presents*~®

 PASSION GUARANTEED SEDUCTION

2 FREE NOVELS PLUS
2 FREE GIFTS!

YES! Please send me 2 FREE Harlequin Presents® novels and my 2 FREE gifts (gifts are worth about $10). After receiving them, if I don't wish to receive any more books, I can return the shipping statement marked "cancel." If I don't cancel, I will receive 6 brand-new novels every month and be billed just $4.05 per book in the U.S. or $4.74 per book in Canada. That's a saving of close to 15% off the cover price! It's quite a bargain! Shipping and handling is just 50¢ per book in the U.S. and 75¢ per book in Canada.* I understand that accepting the 2 free books and gifts places me under no obligation to buy anything. I can always return a shipment and cancel at any time. Even if I never buy another book, the two free books and gifts are mine to keep forever.

106 HDN E4FN   306 HDN E4FY

Name	(PLEASE PRINT)	
Address		Apt. #
City	State/Prov.	Zip/Postal Code

Signature (if under 18, a parent or guardian must sign)

Mail to the **Harlequin Reader Service**:
IN U.S.A.: P.O. Box 1867, Buffalo, NY 14240-1867
IN CANADA: P.O. Box 609, Fort Erie, Ontario L2A 5X3

Not valid for current subscribers to Harlequin Presents books.

Are you a current subscriber to Harlequin Presents books and want to receive the larger-print edition? Call 1-800-873-8635 today!

* Terms and prices subject to change without notice. Prices do not include applicable taxes. N.Y. residents add applicable sales tax. Canadian residents will be charged applicable provincial taxes and GST. Offer not valid in Quebec. This offer is limited to one order per household. All orders subject to approval. Credit or debit balances in a customer's account(s) may be offset by any other outstanding balance owed by or to the customer. Please allow 4 to 6 weeks for delivery. Offer available while quantities last.

Your Privacy: Harlequin Books is committed to protecting your privacy. Our Privacy Policy is available online at www.eHarlequin.com or upon request from the Reader Service. From time to time we make our lists of customers available to reputable third parties who may have a product or service of interest to you. If you would prefer we not share your name and address, please check here. ☐

Help us get it right—We strive for accurate, respectful and relevant communications. To clarify or modify your communication preferences, visit us at www.ReaderService.com/consumerchoice.

HP10

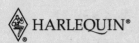

LAURA MARIE ALTOM

The Baby Twins

Stephanie Olmstead has her hands full raising her twin baby girls on her own. When she runs into old friend Brady Flynn, she's shocked to find herself suddenly attracted to the handsome airline pilot! Will this flyboy be the perfect daddy—or will he crash and burn?

HARLEQUIN *Presents*

Coming Next Month

in **Harlequin Presents® EXTRA.** Available April 13, 2010

#97 RICH, RUTHLESS AND SECRETLY ROYAL
Robyn Donald
Regally Wed

#98 FORGOTTEN MISTRESS, SECRET LOVE-CHILD
Annie West
Regally Wed

#99 TAKEN BY THE PIRATE TYCOON
Daphne Clair
Ruthless Tycoons

#100 ITALIAN MARRIAGE: IN NAME ONLY
Kathryn Ross
Ruthless Tycoons

Coming Next Month

in **Harlequin Presents®.** Available April 27, 2010:

#2915 VIRGIN ON HER WEDDING NIGHT
Lynne Graham

#2916 TAMED: THE BARBARIAN KING
Jennie Lucas
Dark-Hearted Desert Men

#2917 BLACKWOLF'S REDEMPTION
Sandra Marton
Men Without Mercy

#2918 THE PRINCE'S CHAMBERMAID
Sharon Kendrick
At His Service

#2919 MISTRESS: PREGNANT BY THE SPANISH BILLIONAIRE
Kim Lawrence

#2920 RUTHLESS RUSSIAN, LOST INNOCENCE
Chantelle Shaw